HUSTLE, BABY

ALSO BY PRIYA GUNS

Your Driver Is Waiting

HUSTLE, BABY

A NOVEL

PRIYA GUNS

DOUBLEDAY NEW YORK

FIRST DOUBLEDAY HARDCOVER EDITION 2026

Published by Doubleday, a division of Penguin Random House LLC, 1745 Broadway, New York, NY 10019.

Doubleday and the portrayal of an anchor with a dolphin are registered trademarks of Penguin Random House LLC.

LIBRARY OF CONGRESS CATALOGING-IN-PUBLICATION DATA
Names: Guns, Priya author
Title: Hustle, baby / Priya Guns.
Description: First Doubleday hardcover edition. |
New York : Doubleday, [2026]
Identifiers: LCCN 2025048964 (print) | LCCN 2025048965 (ebook) |
ISBN 9780385550482 hardcover | ISBN 9780385550499 ebook
Subjects: LCGFT: Fiction | Novels
Classification: LCC PR9199.4.G8645 H87 2026 (print) |
LCC PR9199.4.G8645 (ebook)
LC record available at https://lccn.loc.gov/2025048964
LC ebook record available at https://lccn.loc.gov/2025048965

penguinrandomhouse.com | doubleday.com

Printed in the United States of America
1st Printing

The authorized representative in the EU for product safety and compliance is Penguin Random House Ireland, Morrison Chambers, 32 Nassau Street, Dublin D02 YH68, Ireland, https://eu-contact.penguin.ie.

For my family

Common sense will not accomplish great things.
Simply become insane and desperate.

—*LORD NAOSHIGE*

ACT 1

DILO

A confidence artist knows more than they'll ever tell you. They know how to get what they want when they want it, and they make it look near easy. They're charming. Ten steps ahead, even if you feel like you're the one leading. You'll never know how many truths and how many lies made up their story.

If we reached for the stars and happened to tumble
thank God there was no lava on the moon.

People need something to believe in. Something to hang on to. Something they can call their own. I could tell you about the shrapnel in my mother's chest. I could tell you how the sound of thunder sometimes made me piss myself. Maybe you'd shed a little tear for me. But I was no sob story. We all had our own little sadness. Whatever.

OCTOBER 4, 2000

We were at Z-Mart. A big box chain a twenty-three-minute walk or a ten-minute bus ride away from our house. A national treasure proud of its customer service where the customer was always right even though they had been ripped off a thousand times before reaching the checkout. At store 416 in the Malvern Mall in Scarborough, we were the Nobodies. Hoodlums, alcoholics, white trash, or terrorists—majority immigrant—all of us deemed degenerate. The only service we were offered was plastic cups with morsels they had circulating called *free samples.* The entire store for the month was orange and black, made Halloween spooky.

Anji wore a tight pale yellow shirt with no bra on. You could practically make out the shape and size of her areolae. She knew there were monsters out there, but she was willing to take her chances; after all, she could fire a Kalashnikov and had impeccable aim. She could kill with her bare hands.

Mary wore a bobbled and worn navy jogging set. Her curly hair was brushed to a Sai Baba 'fro. Fifty brush strokes on either side. Mary, so full of grace, born Naagadevi Number One, was a cobra. Yes, that's what I said, the woman who birthed me was also a snake. *Naja naja,* of the family Elapidae. Venomous and capable of preying on their own. Immigrant mom, she was only threatening if you asked her about her stance on homosexuality and public displays of affection. She'd pray for acid rain on the Pride parade but make you a sandwich if you were hungry. Mary held Maysha close to her chest.

Maysha was three foot and three years young. She was cute. Real cute, and cute was the biggest distraction. People had less sympathy for ugly. If you were cute and struggling, for sure the world hated you. A demon child lived in Maysha's belly and made her scream at the top of her lungs. That demon was a pain in my ass.

In the foyer opposite the buggies at the Z-Mart entrance, a little girl in pigtails and an overall dress, with freckles that spotted the top half of her face, stood beside an elderly man wearing an old brown suit, with a red poppy pinned on his chest.

"Spare any change for War Amps?" asked the girl.

"Change for the armed forces?" begged the man.

Terrance was on the other side, standing about six foot. He worked every day except Sundays and had a big belly that was more hard than soft, full of roti and goat curry. His white security shirt was this close to popping if only Terrance sneezed and squeezed his butt. He let out a burp instead. Despite his after-meal lethargy, he mustered every ounce of energy to raise his head ever so slightly, eyeing Anji's tits jiggling with the vibration of the cart.

Rattle
Clank
Clank

"Sign up and get ten percent off your next purchase. A complimentary bag of easing-into-heart-disease included."

"Want a credit card? Who wants a credit card?" The echo of workers selling laminated crack.

If the fact you couldn't afford much made you queasy, there were antacids conveniently located at the end of every aisle. That and all the gum in the world. You could blow bubbles so big you could live in them.

Pop
Pop
Pop

A problem I had was that I couldn't unsee phony. I was sensitive to fake. I had the makings of the world's best bullshit detector. I suffered from acid reflux as a result. Two doctors and a specialist confirmed that I had the amount of acid expected for a forty-five-year-old alcoholic. I was meant to be dead a long time ago. A bunch of us were. We ran straight from bombs to carcinogens and consumerism.

The only creatures who knew peace in this hellhole were the HD fish swimming across flat-screens. Invest in a forty-two-inch and get a pair of subwoofers for 25 percent off. Use your store credit card and receive a free lava lamp and blue headlights. Buy in the next few seconds and a troll will suck your genitals for free.

To the right of Health and Beauty was the first security camera. Loitering in Jewelry was our ticket out of the store scot-free. A woman with rollers in her hair. Her chin was an inch from the glass, her breath fogging her view. She eyed necklaces and brooches. Jewelry designed for women over the hill and rolling. Her purse wide open on the counter.

"Oh my God, it's Sheila," said Mary.

"Who the hell is Sheila?" I asked.

"She owns a penthouse in the condo I work at. What a stylish woman. Look at her. What a beautiful blouse."

Mary swept her shoulder-length bush behind her ears, fondly admiring Sheila from afar.

"What's she doing at this Z-Mart?"

"Our Z-Mart has the best deals of all the Z-Marts. Didn't you know?"

I threw a pack of fruit snacks into the cart. Mary threw in pads, which I'd later stuff in my backpack. I grabbed a bottle of baby shampoo and a bar of soap. Appear as inconspicuous as a citizen who can afford their basic needs.

We dispersed to complete our individual assignments. Maysha was stuck with me and out of control. She stood between men's sweaters hanging from a rack, staring off into the distance. A sudden twinkle in her eye, and she was overcome with a burst of energy, or as Mary would say, that child was possessed by the devil. She sped from Men's Wear to Women's, picking up her pace to a toddler sprint. Cute was as useful as it was annoying. I ran straight for her, passing Mary stuffing bread rolls into her pockets in aisle seven.

"Maysha!" I shouted, weaving through the evening crowd. I spotted Anji in aisle nine.

"I don't think you understand. What I need is to be relieved of all that I feel inside," she said to a store clerk.

A juicy whitehead pulsated on the teenager's nose. He had a tub of Metamucil in his hands.

I was on the move, but it was in my best interest to speed-walk casually. Teenagers wearing hoodies couldn't simply run free. Not with unpaid crap in their bag. I turned a corner toward Electronics.

In front of a whole shelf of screens, there was Maysha standing still, watching an old man in a wheelchair in front of an HD thirty-six-inch plasma TV. In an unnamed drought-ridden land, far away from the cold of this place, crisp on the display, was an African boy with kwashiorkor. He stared directly into the lens. His eyes were round, brown, and captivating. His skin was ashy and gray. Flies hovered around his sores. He scratched his bloated belly. The camera zoomed, narrowing in on his face. A cloud of dust hazed the image.

The old man cried in his wheelchair and Maysha couldn't take her eyes off the man.

"Sir, hang on. Sir?" called a young woman in a bright red Z-Mart shirt. "Just wait right there a second. Sir? Don't go running from me, now. Did you want to try a free sample of the new scented tissues we just got in stock?" She pointed to a display beside the screen.

"Our biscuits will cheer you up," said another woman in a Krafty Kon vest. She held up a plate of samples and handed the old man a serving-sized cup. The old man pawed at the contents, the cup looking smaller in his palm. He balanced the morsel on the tip of his finger and stuffed it in his mouth. He took another cup and did the same. He reached for another, but the woman pulled back the plate.

"Sorry, sir. Company policy. Customers are only allowed one sample."

The man grunted, about to turn and roll away.

"But all right, let's make it your lucky day."

She presented the plate to the man again. He grabbed another cup, throwing the bite down his throat. A flake or a grain tickled the wrong pipe, irritating the man's esophagus. He coughed. And he coughed. Crumbs flew on the woman's face. At Z-Mart, the customers were always right, so the woman smiled.

I grabbed Maysha by the hood of her coat. We caught up with Anji, pushing our cart as we casually scoped for Mary. I headed toward Jewelry. The bag of the woman Mary said was named Sheila was still open on the counter. Her face was squished against the glass.

"Wouldn't expect this sort of quality for the price, that's for sure," she said to the Jewelry saleswoman.

"So very, ma'am."

"You don't think this looks tacky? Be honest."

"No, ma'am. *So* nice."

I peeked into the woman's bag as I walked by, feigning interest in a set of friendship bracelets. Lipstick, hand cream, vaginal spray. I slipped in a ninety-five-dollar bottle of cologne under a silk handkerchief.

At the checkout, our cashier's skin was dry from counting money. She had paper cuts on her fingers from opening rolls of coins in a hurry as she watched the line from her checkout meander into Pantry Goods every day well after closing time. Mary bagged our shopping, keeping her arms awkwardly to her side. Attempting to hide the items behind her coat in her bespoke pockets.

Anji eyed our total. Dollar after dollar. She bit her thumb.

Five items left to scan. I still had a clear view of Sheila from our checkout. She pulled out her credit card as our cashier scanned a pack of tea biscuits. Just as our cashier grabbed the box of nuggets, Anji stopped her with her hand.

"We don't need the last three items, please," she whispered to the cashier across the register.

The clerk put the goods to the side. Conveniently for us, Maysha was preoccupied. She was drawn to a newly installed screen. Krafty Kon Koyote dancing with a Nail Gun Pro—the millennium edition—shooting nails into a crowd of colored Mylar balloons. *The tool for every workingman.* Everyone had a Nail Gun Pro, like everyone had the crap on sale at Z-Mart each week.

We grabbed our bags. I led the way, managing our speed, until Sheila was exactly in front of us nearing the exit. In a moment, I saw her catch Mary's eye. Mary smiled but Sheila walked off, nearing the sensor. Five, four, three, two—the alarm sounded.

"Excuse me, ma'am," called Terrance, hoisting himself off his chair.

"There must be a mistake," whined Sheila, quickly digging through her bag, handing Terrance her receipt, finding the box of ninety-five-dollar cologne, unpaid for.

The four of us were out the door with a savings of ninety-nine seventy-five.

MARY

English isn't my first language. To call it my second, ha, how terrible was second place? Translation required an understanding of culture, you see. Of people. Of history. Of too much to list and explain. For example, if I wanted to be stern with my daughter, I might have said, *"You dark dirty dog, if you don't do well in school, I'll grab you by the neck and bash your head against the wall to find out, once and for all, if you were born with a brain."*

I sound like a monster, no? Ha! I'm laughing. That's just our love, no? We don't really mean everything we say. Our children understood the difference because we *showed* our love. You see? *Verry* big difference. I like simple things. I don't care for the big or spectacular. I wouldn't say that I ever asked for much. Yes, I grew up with servants, but I went out and played and climbed trees even though it made my mother anxious. I was a rebel in my own way. I could fire a slingshot. That was my knack. Knock down some jackfruit and mangoes in a single shot. I used to wear dresses. Beautiful frocks that showed off my legs, but if you saw my knees you'd know that I played football and jumped fences. I didn't care for school. I liked fishing and playing netball, swinging from branches on our banyan tree. I wasn't allowed to do much, now that I remember, but absolutely that made me want to do everything I was told I couldn't.

I missed our fruit. Those blossoms in the spring. Summer citrus bursting. Putrefying flesh. Stinging sickly sweet. Ha! What else? The sun gave me headaches. The tide played Carnatic chords. The smell of the Indian Ocean was too fishy for me. I may be the only person you meet of my generation repulsed by a bowl of odiyal kool. But don't stretch this into some pitiful story. I feel that's what you people do. I come from paradise, that's true. But it was a place with venomous snakes, land mines, and bullets flying. There wasn't a single family who didn't know a person who died from a snakebite or two. There wasn't a single family who didn't know a person who'd been killed.

My husband was a biology lecturer, but my father, the magistrate, would've preferred if he worked for the embassy. But Kannan loved me even with my "broken tongue and brain," is how he teased me. He couldn't afford biriyani some days. His father sold appum from his cart in the mornings. His mother swept the sides of the road. So, Kannan couldn't afford to buy me gold. Not even on our wedding day.

A thaali is a golden necklace husbands gift their prizes. Sorry, brides. Almost like a dowry, but in reverse, financial security in the guise of a loving gift. Could even be worth $25,000, a quarter of a lakh. My father gifted me two golden bracelets and a thaali that had people down our lane talking. My father and brother were taken hostage during the pogroms in '57. They survived, thank God. But they were beaten *verry* badly.

OCTOBER 6

I was in prayer seated at the edge of my bed with a notice from our landlord beside me. The Tamil Radio, which ran 24/7, played softer than usual that day. There was no shutting off the thing. My suitcase was between my feet. I pulled it from under the bed, patting the leather like it was my favorite ox when I was a child—Ox 43, who never shied from showing off his iron branding.

As I unbuckled the straps and unzipped my suitcase, I remembered as usual that monsoon evening I filled each corner with all I thought we needed for our move. Clothing, a photo album, brand-new socks. Then, in front of me, all that was deemed *verry* important. Documents. Certificates. Proof of landing. I kept my father's hanky, which was wrapped around my gold, neatly tucked in the folds of my silk Kanchipuram sari. Every item as I had left them. I pushed my suitcase back under the bed.

What to do? What to do? That was all I was thinking.

I made paruppu. I burned rice. I warmed some leftovers

and plated them on the table. Our purple maple tree still had leaves. Dilo's target board was brought closer to the house from the back fence. Her aim was always improving. Anji had taught the girl how to shoot. How to fight. Rebellion ran in our blood, or Anji had passed it down through all of her stories. *Chi!* I wish she had taught Dilo how to clean instead. Dilo had used old report cards, past-due notices, pictures of brands and leaders she called "evil," all target faces for their fun. Can you imagine the extra worries I had? A niece and her aunt had a bond of their own, no? The two as individuals were handfuls, and as a pair, my God! Only Jesus could save them.

What to do? What to do?

I sat at the kitchen table, still in my yellow robe. I placed the notice between a plate of rice and a bowl of fried bitter melon.

The tinkling sound of fifty bells smaller than a lentil entered the room. Anji's anklets. The best way for us to know when she was near. She marched into the kitchen.

"Bloody hell. Dilo! Dilo!"

Dilo ran from the living room wearing baggy basketball shorts I'd tried throwing away twice. Her sweater was Hugo Boss, at least, which she had found brand-new on the bus, she said.

"Yo, man! I was watching TV."

"You didn't do the dishes."

"I just told you. I was *watching* TV. I'm with Maysha, man."

"Did you give her food? Did she eat?"

"She said she wasn't hungry."

"She doesn't understand what her body needs. Maysha! Maysha! Maysha, come here," called Anji.

I felt their shadows over me. I shut my eyes, turning more toward the wall. I let them speak. My burnt rice. The watery paruppu. Scraps of keerai on a saucer. Rasam made with "no love," as Dilo often said when the food I prepared with my aching hands wasn't good enough for them.

"How long have you just sat here, akka? Akka. Akka? I'm talking to you. How long have you just sat here?"

"What do you mean, just sat here? Do you not see the food in front of you?"

Anji turned toward the counter. She clicked through the callers on the phone display. Dilo opened the fridge. Maysha pulled Dilo's arm. Anji paced. Back and forth. Up and down. That's what she did. When a situation was more wrong than right, that was her dance. I covered my eyes with my hands.

Wahhhhh!

Her child began screaming. Screaming. The way that child screamed. She screamed like only children in this country can.

"Nuggets! Nuggets!"

In Jesus's name. I held my tongue.

"We got no nuggets, freak. Want a banana? It's brown but still yummy."

I peeked through my fingers. Dilo handed Maysha a banana. The slow rot of flesh and sugar. Maysha tried to peel the top. She moaned. She groaned. She screamed again.

Wahhhhh!

"Put the banana in a bowl. Pour condensed milk. Get two spoons. Dilo and Maysha. Get out of my misery. Go!" I shouted.

Maysha rubbed away the single tear she forced down to her cheek. Dilo rolled her eyes. Her jaundiced complexion. The hairs on her upper lip. Her crooked teeth. Dark girls had fewer prospects. Anji returned from her panicked dance conveniently after her child's needs were met and the children were no longer in the kitchen.

"What is this?" She picked up the notice from the table, calculating immediately.

Due to excessive recurrent late payments we require all months' rent for the duration of the year to be paid by 9 a.m. on December 15. Tenants will be required to vacate the property if total payment cannot be made. Failure to cooperate will result in immediate legal action.

"We'll have enough to pay for August and the last two weeks of July with your next paycheck."

"With my next paycheck?" I asked.

"We can't afford any more late payments, and we need to be caught up by the fifteenth of December. What day is it today?"

"Can we manage?"

"Nine hundred for August and September, five hundred for July, plus this month and up to December—what does that work out to?"

"Five thousand dollars, not including food, expenses, and all of my stress. Aiyo kadavuley! How are we this much behind? What happened to your money?" I asked.

Anji huffed. Anji puffed. We kept a nail gun in the bottom drawer for when the house was falling down, for when the foundation was giving up. She pulled the sliding back door open with the gun in her hand. Balanced. Still. She took a breath and pulled the trigger.

Tuck
Tuck
Tuck

Three nails hit the shooting board.

"Why do you look like that?" she asked me, putting the gun away.

"What do you mean? What do I look like?"

"Like you haven't had any sugar for days. I know when you wish you were dead."

"I had some grapes," I told her. "I had grapes maybe two hours ago."

I stood from my chair to make us some tea as Anji looked out into the backyard. The tea we drank was the color of our mother's favorite Bata slippers. When we were naughty, she would throw her slippers at us. She aimed for our faces. I put a cup of tea for Anji on the table. I told her to sit down.

"Don't tell me. Don't tell me. Look at me, akka . . . they laid you off. Did they? Did they lay you off at the condo? Bloody hell. I knew something was wrong."

The modern women in our house, even with all the language and imagery made available to them, deliberately chose the filthiest words to use in my presence.

"Did they give you your holiday pay? They need to pay your severance, akka. Are you sure you were paid all of your overtime hours? Akka, do you see those bills beside the telephone?"

Anji suffered from her lack of faith. She had pimples on her back because of it.

"I will do what I always do. I will pray. That's all I can do, and I can only do what I can."

Anji rolled her eyes. That's how Anji was. She thought she could solve every problem, that she would do well on her own, that she didn't need God because if He was so merciful how could He allow all this suffering. For a philosophical mind, she understood God in simple terms. Anji didn't fear God's wrath. Anji didn't believe in His mercy. God spoke to Moses through a burning bush, and He made a donkey speak to Balaam. What more can I say? Dilo had said I was the real con artist, but she didn't understand my faith, either. The woman and girls in our house didn't fear God, and that was our problem. I prayed for them daily.

ANJI

I was a Tamil woman born in the year 1963. Though I was most often seen in camouflage and combat boots, I enjoyed wearing short skirts and tight, fitted trousers. I showed my legs and my shoulders. A little cleavage sometimes and my midriff on special occasions through sheer lace saris. I also had friends born with penises. I whistled. Laughed loudly. Danced and made crude jokes with friends, including any men in my life. For all of these reasons I was called a whore. Terrible, isn't it?

The Terms and Conditions for Having a Child. I should've written out a legal document. I never expected a pregnancy in my thirties, and I never tried. I found men embarrassing to be in public with. I worried about hormonal imbalances. Potential complications. The terror of pushing out a child or an incision along the torso. Hearing myself scream as my vagina was ripped apart. The infinite ways the baby could die.

Dead baby
Dead baby
Still and dismembered on the roadside.

I was not prepared for the literal and figurative evidence that I had been "fucked"—as they say—and forever "fucked over," by a chimp in a suit. A chimp who would at some point disappoint, embarrass, and hurt me, if he hadn't already. Necking whores with names like Crossandra as I nursed and cleaned his baby's bottom. Shit and piss all over me.

No matter; the greatest day of my life was when I gave birth to my baby, Maysha.

I worked as an insurance broker in a twenty-story building *downtown*. The only place that hired me with decent pay. If I'd had the opportunity of choice, I'd have taught philosophy, for which I got my degree. I was hired in '91. A year after Dilo and Mary arrived.

The building was gray and white and drab. Imagine a prison with the bars removed. Fresh white paint over concrete and water stains. A very distinct pine-scented cleaning fluid. Classic motivational posters. A cat hanging on a laundry line. Neil Armstrong on the moon. Bill Gates and Mother Teresa holding hands and tonguing, and a painting of a motley star, because that's what we were to our team.

One day in the staff room after lunch, eating alone on

a bar stool facing the window, I noticed a yellow card pinned on the bulletin board.

Give it your all!
Managerial positions will be announced next week.
Have you met your targets?

I marched to the stationery desk and grabbed a black marker.

We'll blow this place to smithereens!

My period was due, which mattered to no one. Within six hours, I received a complaint from HR. Straight to my email. Not even a call or a tap on my shoulder. I was a "terrorist." That's what they called me. I was spreading communist propaganda. And if I wasn't, I was a sympathizer, guilty of spreading hate.

For my "outburst," I was given a warning. So, I started arriving at the office half an hour earlier than expected. I had coffee dripping fresh from the filter by the time staff arrived. I was the first or second smile anyone saw in that building.

Kumar Gupta was his name. A man with a wife and kids and fifteen-plus years with the company. He slapped my backside one sunny day in July. I made a complaint, but only after grabbing him by the neck and smashing his head into the wall. Somehow, I was the one they let go on that very day.

A leak in the bathroom. A window that wouldn't shut. A kid for a fussy eater or a fussy eater for a kid. A teenager I believed sold marijuana from her locker. A sister who was laid off. I was jobless for three months and kept my business private. I was home to catch Dilo cutting cubes of butter on the kitchen counter. She wrapped each serving in Saran wrap. Trimming the edges and neatly tucking the extra plastic. Two weeks later, when the new school year started, her principal, Mr. Nixon, called. Dilo sold those same serving-sized squares of butter for a quarter in the cafeteria. She sold packets of ketchup, mustard, and relish to children on the playground at a nearby elementary school. One of those children was only five. Dilo sold that poor child a packet of ketchup for ten dollars.

Like many families, Mary and I wanted to have more time at home with our children, but we had to work to *keep* our family. A single day off could throw a whole month into disarray. God forbid, we had a family emergency and had to take time off? Never.

Don't open the door
Don't answer the phone
Don't touch the stove
Don't talk to strangers

Our children took care of each other as best they could in our absence. But there we were. My sister and I, at home, unemployed, with zero savings.

"Where are you going? Sit down. Will you call the job agency for me?" asked akka, seated at the kitchen table, looking down at her mug. I couldn't listen to her for longer than seven minutes. The simple fact was that every time Mary spoke about her God, I was losing brain cells. Losing the will to survive.

"I need a break from this," I said, stepping from the chair. I grabbed my silver tin of rollies and a lighter from the utility drawer. I took my mug of tea to the porch, where the sky that evening was lavender, and Dilo stood facing the road. An owl nestled within a cavity of our neighbor's pine tree.

Dilo had our machete in her hand, slashing at our front bushes on the lawn. "Dilo! What are you doing? You already know, you use the machete in the backyard. Bring it here! Do you want the neighbors to go mad?"

"I'm pruning the cedar, man. I practice the swipes—*you* taught me—in the backyard, behind the maple tree. I'm not a fucking dumbass, dude."

"You're lucky there's not a boot here."

She swung the machete at her side walking over. Slouching. I worried she was self-conscious about her breasts. Mary teased her often. She wasn't large chested, only a teenager growing into her new body.

"Maysha took a dump behind the couch," she said, rubbing her chin, resting the machete against the brick wall of our house, on the porch.

“Oh Christ. Again?”

“I cleaned it up. Don’t worry.”

She grabbed a tennis ball out of a shoe. She threw it against the brick wall. Something she’d done since we first moved, back when her hand could hardly wrap around the ball.

I exhaled. Shamelessly, I found comfort in smoking. The sound of my breath. My stress leaving. Leaving. Gone, but not forever.

“I might be winning five hundred dollars soon,” said Dilo, catching the ball and throwing it again.

“What do you mean?”

“I have a feeling I’m about to win an essay contest.”

“Is that so?”

“Maybe. Who knows. I better. I’ll give you guys the money.”

“Sure. All right.”

“. . . You know that lady who lives by the catwalk?” she continued.

“Monty Dame or Drucilla?”

“The one whose husband left her wandering in her robe every night for a month.”

“Monty Dame. I saw her drinking with some men at the Z-Mart parking lot two weeks ago.”

“She’s been driving round the block in a pink Caddy for the past few minutes. She must be doing all right now.”

Dilo missed the ball, and it rolled down our driveway, swerving and stopping on our lawn, under the bushes. She ran over to fetch her ball and, just as she said, there was Ms. Monty Dame driving ten miles an hour. Smooth, in a pink 1990 DeVille. The sticker still on the window. Her hair blown out so every layer could be marveled at. French tips and silver rings. A box diamond on a white gold band. A Tiffany bracelet with stiletto charms. She listened to Barenaked Ladies.

Dilo hailed her down and walked over to the road, with her tennis ball in her hand. Monty rolled down her window, smacking a wad of purple gum in her mouth.

"Sick ride," said Dilo.

"Real nice, ain't it?" Monty beamed.

"Got a CD player?"

"It plays CDs right in there. You got music for me to listen to?"

"Ten bucks a mix."

I peered inside the car.

"Hello, Miss Pretty Kitty. You get a good gander?"

"How'd you get this car, Monty?" I asked.

"Can't even say hi and you ain't shy, don't we all know it."

"Oh, shut up."

"Take this extra coffee, will ya? Ordered two at Mona's by mistake. Paid for the two anyway."

A gold Casio around her wrist. The wrinkles on her hands. Her blush a new terra-cotta rose. A few units of Botox in her forehead. Her eyebrow pencil was the perfect texture for her skin. Her lipstick bled from the pencil line she'd traced around her lips, and my hopes plunged deep into her neckline, along her thin skin. She handed me a coffee through the passenger window.

"How'd you get the car, Monty?" I asked again.

"Gary Elle, honey. The world's fifth-best direct-selling brand of skin care and cosmetics. Changed my life. You gotta join. Be part of the movement. Start your own business too, sweetie, I bet you're a natural. That's the only way to bring up the kids and be who you are these days, you know what I mean?"

She had veneers and a gold canine cap. I wasn't sure if she had on the latest WonderBra or had gotten breast implants. How quick did such surgeries heal? Her cleavage was up to her chin.

"Anji said you were sniffing gas like a week ago," said Dilo, brushing some dirt off Monty's front light.

Monty Dame chuckled, nearly choking on her gum. You could hear from the phlegm in her chest she'd been smoking since she was a teen.

"Women like us gotta stick together, hon. Give me a call and let's get you started. Only takes a couple days."

She handed me a sharp card from a stack she had in a cup holder. Soft white, embossed letters, styled with gold filigree.

"It's the year 2000, honey. We should be living our dreams."

Monty winked, still smacking that wad of purple gum in her mouth. She drove off and round the block another twenty times, playing her music loudly.

DILO

When Mary was Naga Devi Number One, she used to sit on the edge of a cliff and look down at the Jaffna Lagoon. Ever since I was born, she took me with her. Coconut in one hand, machete in the other.

I was six in 1991. Just a few months before we left to live where the temperature could drop as low as twenty-three below with the windchill. Damn cold is what I mean. The women in my grandma's house were on the rattan chairs in the living room. The concrete floor was brick red and worn. It left a crimson dusting on the soles of your feet. The women were Mary before she was Mary: Pathma the servant girl, Kutti chiththi, and my ammamma—my grandma—who sat cross-legged on the rug cutting pumpkin with her machete. Pathma snapped beans she threw into a pot stable on her lap. I don't know where my appa was but, whatever. Maama was in the kitchen stirring meen kulambu.

A BANG. A howl. Another dark night.

Ammamma held her blade. She was the first out the door. Maama followed with a broom. Mary, before she was Mary, and her sister, not Anji but Kutti chiththi, they ran behind. Old Man Shiva passed along on his rickety bicycle. He pushed through the fog. Through the haze.

Caw, caw, went the crow in the jackfruit tree.

A demon ran toward us. His arms hung from sinews of flesh. Chunks of his torso fell to the ground. His skin was charred, smelling of rubber. His eyes were holes through his skull.

"They poured petrol on him! Those bastards poured petrol on my brother!"

A woman ran over. She collapsed outside the house. The women of my family ran to console her. They held her. They cried. The demon ran toward the Indian Ocean.

The ceiling fan spun, clattering. I'd never know where my appa was, but Mary and I were on our backs on our mattress on the floor. I wondered if the fan would fall and slice our heads off. Mary turned over to me. She couldn't sleep either. Stroking the wet hairs on my forehead, she let out a sigh before turning onto her back again. A gecko scurried on the wall after a fly, and the room was sticky.

"A million horrors have happened on this land for centuries and it's possible to feel them all in a single night," she said in Tamil.

That was the first of the few times Mary made any sense to me.

OCTOBER 9

As far back as I remember, I was a hustler. Hustling was in my blood because my cells formed in times of shelling, and my mother had to run so we didn't die that day.

When I started my business ventures in the ninth grade, I had no choice but to be a showman. If you're anything like me, you gotta learn the skill of fitting in just enough so you're not on anyone's radar. A few seconds was all you had to get someone's attention. I had business cards, which helped. Printed them on A4 copy paper. Font. Layout. Scrupulously selected on Microsoft Paint.

The school buses dropped off hordes of students at 8 a.m., and the 134 pulled up just after. Teenagers with empty stomachs dreading first lesson was *prime time* for a savvy salesman like me. I stood on the bench outside the public bus stop, a bag of snacks and juice boxes ready. Cans of cold coffee. All Krafty Kon, so trusted by many. Working with a limited supply to spike demand. I lacked the luxury of "just in time" inventory, but there I was, and the kids called me Hustle Baby.

> *"Let's sort the doers from the slackers, the hungry from the snackers, those who trust me from the ones who don't, because if you didn't have breakfast this morning, you won't pass class—hell, you won't pass gas. You'll be coming back right here, to restart the ninth grade. Who wants cereal bars, right this way!?"*

Make kids laugh, and they'll remember you. Kept them rolling back to me the next day, and the day after. Kids in other schools were singing my jingle. I built my own clientele. Stacked shelves in my locker. Put up hooks and displays. CDs. DVDs. Big fan of movies. VHS pornos. Printed and bound copies of *No Logo*. Snacks. A cooler. I had a cooler. I sold ice-cold drinks all year long. I had anything you needed on sale.

I stood against my locker. A boy walked over, a customer of mine, waddling in his extra-baggy jeans. Aqua bandana hanging from his back pocket. Aqua because that was his crew's color. They should've picked a tougher color. Malvern's Brown Boys Styling. They should have picked a better name. Riding around in Civics with gats and machetes, unafraid to chop a guy. These guys knew war. Some of them knew it yesterday. Freshies usually had stories no one could fuck with.

"Got any PlayStation games, Hustle Baby?"

"All right. Keep it down."

"Lemme get *Knockout Kings* and a bag of Doritos."

My English teacher, Ms. Lieberman, was heading out of her classroom. I made the deal quick, as discreetly as possible; slammed my locker; clasped the lock; and ran down the hall after her.

"Miss. Miss. Did you read my essay, miss? Do you think I stand a shot?"

I'd envisioned this moment in the shower a hundred times, and like an idiot I was more hopeful in each imagining. Ms. Lieberman smiling, close to tears, struggling to voice how much my essay moved her. Nobel Prize–worthy. Gifted child. *New York Times* kid submission. Interviews with Barbara Walters, Larry King, and Oprah Winfrey.

"We'll have to have a talk with Mr. Nixon about your submission, young lady," she said, shaking her head in disappointment. She walked off as if her words didn't poke me. As if I didn't spend hours formulating my thoughts, forging ideas—sharpening words and crafting sentences—setting fire to everything wrong with the world. Safe to say our interaction didn't play out like it had in my head.

MARY

Kannan had black eyes. His skin was perfectly dark for a man. So polished you would think he rubbed butter on himself. He used petroleum jelly. He was spectacularly handsome, but I never told him that. A man mustn't know how you really feel. He must even wonder if you find him attractive. Kannan didn't need compliments. What he needed was to give me attention. He preferred wasting his time in the library instead. Writing papers nobody read.

A man tells you he loves you. That there is no one like you around. You think he'll be the one crying at your funeral, but he'll be the reason you're in the ground.

I had always wanted children even if I didn't know where babies came from. How they formed in the womb. I didn't pay attention in science class, and no one bothered to tell me. I dreamed of having ten daughters. Oiling and brushing and plaiting their hair. I'd line them up in the garden, dressed in frocks. Look at these beautiful daughters I made. They'd marry rich and handsome men, and we'd travel around the world hand in hand. I'd have a nice bag. I'd wear silk trousers. Ha! I'm laughing. I used to dream foolishly; now I dream only of a warm winter coat.

OCTOBER 10

The kitchen was tidy. Tea was in a pot. I made rava lattu for the girls, shaping each into a ball in my hands. The rubbish was heavy. I carried the bags out by myself. Secure in each respective bin. My God, the way the toilet sparkled. The grime in the shower. I nearly broke my back. Laundry was loaded and folded. Placed back in the correct drawer. Placed back on the right shelf. I prayed and gave my devotion to the Lord. I felt a terrible sadness. So, I sat with a cup of tea.

"Maysha, I've told you a thousand times, you can't have whatever you want. Life doesn't work that way."

Anji walked in from the living room. That woman left the television playing. She held Maysha on her hip, bouncing to soothe her. Maysha's cheeks were red, her lips swollen from crying. Her grumpy face. Her button nose. "But I want one—" she cried, nestling her head on her mother's shoulder. Anji rubbed her back. Rocking back and forth. That woman was my younger sister.

"We already have a Nail Gun Pro, chellam. We don't need the millennium edition. You have to eat something now."

Maysha shut her eyes.

"Look. How about some lattu. There's lattu. Have lattu."

Maysha tucked her lips from even tasting, snuggling against her mother's neck, still resting on her shoulder.

"You wanted to talk about something?" I finally asked. My voice cracked from hours of not speaking.

"I'm a little busy. Can you make us tea?"

"There's tea in the pot," I said.

Without a glance at the steaming pot, the cup and saucer left for her on the counter with two Italian ladyfingers on a plate, while rubbing Maysha's spine, Anji carried Maysha back to the living room.

The Tamil Radio played a segment on our victory in Elephant Pass earlier that year, followed by an interview with Muralitharan on how to bowl with rocket success. Dilo hadn't said a word to me in twenty-one hours. She came in smelling of the autumn leaves, dressed like a rowdy. I knew she had been playing with her machete.

"I told you to be careful with the knife, it's not a toy," I said, holding the warm cup. Noticing my daughter's dry face as she kicked her boots off by the door.

"Does it look like I'm bleeding?" she asked, heading to the fridge and swinging the door open.

"I made lattu. On the counter. There's chicken on a plate. You need to put gingelly oil on your skin at night."

Dilo pulled my Tupperware from the fridge. She waved it in the air. I worried the lid would slip. My seeds would fall. Only I and my Lord knew how much bleach I used to scrub the floor.

"Why the hell is there pomegranate?"

"That's my pomegranate."

"Your pomegranate cost five dollars. Did you even make five dollars this week? You bought a pomegranate two days ago. Don't spend money we don't have. For fucksakes!"

Dilo threw my Tupperware in the fridge and shut the fridge door. Her socks were damp. Her feet left moist prints on the linoleum floor. The slam of her bedroom door shook the jar of achchaaru on the kitchen table.

"What happened to her?" asked Anji. She unclasped her bra and pulled it out from her sleeve, throwing the lace on the table.

"What do I know? Will you tell me about the boxes in the living room? All that crab—"

"Crap," corrected Anji.

"Why did Monty call the other day?"

Anji held a lattu. A ball of toasted semolina, raisins, cashews, and sugar pressed with fatty ghee. She took a bite and pulled an ugly face. She spat out the glob in her palm and dumped the slobber in the rubbish bin.

"Salt. Did you think it was sugar? I need a glass of milk."

I grabbed two silver tumblers. She grabbed the pitcher from the fridge, but the milk bag was empty. I had a full bag in my hand ready. She cut a small triangle at the top corner. She poured. We sat down at the kitchen table.

"Will you just tell me? I saw Monty. That car she drove. How much do you think it costs? One lakh, maybe?"

"Seventy grand. But she won it. A prize for star commission."

Anji pushed the tumbler aside, resting her head in her arms on our table.

"You didn't sell a thing, though, did you? It's been two days. How much commission did Monty make in a week to get her car?"

Anji studied her fingernails. Her tongue pressed against her upper lip.

"How did you manage to put salt in the lattu? The sugar is in its own container. The salt is in the shaker. Did you grab the box of salt from the top cupboard? Or did you shake the salt in using the shaker? For the amount of salt in those lattu, you would've been shaking for five minutes. I really don't understand how you managed to do that."

"I'm telling you something. Tracey called. Did you know that?"

"Tracey? What did she want? Did she change her mind?"

"You went selling her products? That's what you did. That's what she told me. All those lipsticks and creams. Stacey is my friend."

"Tracey, you mean."

"*Tracey* is my friend. The only true friend I have on our block."

"Because she trusts you with her sedan? The two of you sitting like heifers on her couch watching TV. Do you think if her husband was alive, she'd give you that much time?"

"Do you think if Jeevan wasn't shot, he'd still be with you? You think he wouldn't have come to know who you really are?"

Anji squeezed my thigh, digging her nails into my skin.

"Po-di vesi." I threw her hand from me.

I got up for some water. I poured Anji a glass. The fridge rumbled. The red light on the phone flashed. We had a voice message. A reminder from our landlord that we had till December 15 to catch up on rent.

"I started a business," said Anji, after taking a sip of water. "If I sign up at least five people, that's two hundred commission for each. That's my objective, more than selling products, you see? There's endless ways of making money if you know the right people."

"But you have no friends."

"Oh, shut up."

"You need to ask God to fix your face, Anji."

She rolled her eyes. I called Dilo.

"Dilo!" I shouted again. "Get my diary. Hurry. Please. Get my diary. I need it now."

She slammed every drawer and door on her way into the kitchen. She handed me my diary, putting it in my hand, knowing if she threw it across the table, I'd twist her arm in half. I handed my diary to Anji.

"When was the last time you prayed?"

"Not now, akka."

"Turn to the page with the 'C' for my church friends. There should be a list. Only God's people can help you, Anji."

The Tamil Radio played thirty minutes of poetry from the books of Bharathi. I went to my room and sat on my bed.

MAYSHA

Maysha struggled to poo, could hardly count to ten, but knew a great purchase when she saw one. She couldn't distinguish letters from numbers, but she knew brands and logos magnetically. Chrome was her favorite color. Infomercials her favorite programming. When Maysha played pretend, an index card became a credit card, and money was infinite. She imagined her nails were long and polished. She was a pretty young woman with pretty-young-woman things, and her name may as well have been Stacey.

The television screen was static. Maysha stood on her tiny bitty feet and jiggled the cable wire at the back of the television, which ran and dipped out of the window and into a box in front of a boy named Yoga's house, where many families connected to free cable. Maysha hit the top of the television, then smacked it once more until the picture was clear again. She sat back on her favorite patch of curly carpet, in front of that television set, in the dark, at night, alone.

ANJI

Akka converted to Christianity on Dilo's third birthday. A month after I left the island in '88. Kannan was an atheist. A scientist by profession. He was also a Jaffna man, so he thought he was right about everything. I believe akka wanted something of her own. Something her husband had no part in because she had no part in much of his world. He kept her, didn't he? As most men keep their women.

My sister grew up climbing trees, and then maybe, as the eldest girl, she felt the pressure to marry, to love, to birth children. She defied our father and changed her name, and she defied her husband by accepting an ideology that claimed his science was a hoax.

I spent time with Dilo when she was a baby. Holding her in a bathroom with twelve others. Waiting for the sound of thunder to stop. Waiting for the song of flying foxes.

I moved to Toronto that September. I moved to Scarborough more specifically, in Malvern to be exact. I was insistent about staying where I was in the North, Back Home, I mean, with my people. But the Sri Lankan army shot my lover in the head and then beat him with the back of a G3. My revolutionary, he was. My puppy. My sweet darling puppy. They'd build roads over our bones and cover our ashes with sand.

So-and-so is missing.
Remember the aunty down Pondicherry Lane?
They found her leg in a well.
Do you know one of your boys killed another innocent civilian?
Killed one of our own.
What are your thoughts on the Central Bank attack in Colombo?
What about the civilians?
How could you truly care if you're not there anymore?

"We are born with the sin nature," akka would tell me.
"We are all foul scum!" I'd reply.

Before Miguel Childs was Pastor Childs, we met at a dance party. I don't remember what I wore, but I remember feeling like a kitten. He said he'd noticed the shape of my thighs; that was the first thing he said to me, before we danced together that night. He was coy. Modest for a man as handsome as he was.

"I could never forget a face like yours" was the first thing he said to me when he saw me a second time.

Eventually, we met up for coffee. Had a nice laugh and we started writing letters to each other, which we passed through friends, since we had trouble catching each other on a landline. I'd spray the perfume I wore that day onto the paper, inspiring Miguel's filthy lines.

Is there an inch of you that isn't beautiful?

Lines that picked me up days later.

One cold night, I thought Miguel and I would be intimate, and I needed a physical mauling with a man I felt safe with, a man I was attracted to. We were to meet at seven. Minus twenty-one degrees outside and I wasn't accustomed to the cold. I waited at the Kiss and Pick Up at Kennedy Station wearing a short dress and thigh-high stockings. My cheetah-print coat, which was more stylish than warm. But Miguel didn't show up like he had said he would. I kicked myself for even bothering. He never called to explain what had happened. He never wrote to me again.

I'd been to akka's church on Industrial Drive, but only for their Christmas carol services, and on Easter once or twice. A couple years ago, I found akka sobbing uncontrollably on the couch. Maysha was about a year old at that time and sleeping.

"What happened?" I asked Mary. "Is somebody dead?"

"Our pastor. The founding pastor at Industrial Drive announced his immediate resignation. He's moving to Myrtle Beach with a woman named Marigold. Maybe every word he said was a lie."

Mary cried and cried.

My hope in life was not to find meaning or love, but to find living bearable. I promised akka I'd visit her church when the new pastor was selected. I told her matters would resolve and she'd be all right. Well, on the Sunday I promised to be in attendance, I arrived a little more than fashionably late. I strutted into the sanctuary during a prayer, and who did I see at the pulpit in a well-tailored suit, snug at the crotch? Miguel Childs was now Pastor Childs, with a Bible in his hand.

"Turn to the page with the 'C' for my church friends . . . Only God's people can help you, Anji."

Miguel crossed my mind. Of course he did. But I had a business to run. We were months behind in rent. Miguel had wasted my time once, and that was enough for me. I knew better. I always had.

DILO

It was Friday the thirteenth.

From the window behind Principal Nixon's desk, a band of light filtered through, illuminating a grubby five-dollar bill next to an open envelope on the rug. On the edge of the desk was a toppled tote bag, stuffed with ninth graders' signed permission slips and money for a field trip to the zoo. Principal Nixon had been running his mouth for some time. Yappity. Yappity. Yap. I'd stopped listening a while ago, his yapping drowned out by the gurgling of the acid in my stomach.

Ms. Lieberman stood to the right side of Principal Nixon in that too-tight pencil skirt she wore too often. She wore a silk blouse. I don't remember the color. Arms crossed, looking real pissed about something that, to be honest, wasn't a big deal.

Mary was called into our meeting and sat beside me in a wooden chair. I knew she was only concerned about *appearing* as concerned as possible. She had no idea what was going on. I hoped she'd be on my side for once, bare her fangs in my defense, but I worried she'd side with the authorities. Whatever.

"... you've been an honor roll student, Dilo. I hope you understand the gravity of the situation here. You used a *very* offensive word in your essay, which violates our school's Code of Conduct as well as endangers your fellow students' emotional safety. We have no choice but to disqualify you from the Bright Minds Scarborough High School Essay Competition. We were very disappointed to see something like this from such a promising student. What were you thinking, do you not see that sign?"

All I could think about was how Principal Nixon's arms looked like encased sausages in his snug corduroy blazer, as he pointed to the ZERO TOLERANCE FOR PREJUDICE poster on the back of his door. *I don't read educational-propagandist materials, fat-ass,* is what I would've said, if I wanted a suspension. Instead, I just stared blankly at the guy. Only, slightly above his shoulder. My lazy eye trick, to confuse and startle.

"Zero tolerance for bullying, violence, and slurs. Zero tolerance, Dilo," he said, crossing his chubby arms across his chest.

"But did you read the entire essay, Mr. Nixon? The word in question was used strategically and with great consideration. Only twice, even. My bibliography helps explain. *Gulliver's Travels*—the yahoos. *A Confederacy of Dunces*. *Manufacturing Consent*. Links to the websites I found online—"

"Conspiracy forums don't count," interrupted Ms. Lieberman, raising her hand swiftly. She probably gave Mr. Nixon a Monica Lewinsky on his velvet maroon couch. In that pencil skirt. Her stupid face.

"You wanted our speculations for the future, miss. I wrote a thoughtful warning."

"I don't understand," interrupted Mary. "What is the problem? Dilo is bullying children?"

"I've been wondering, Ms. Kannan. Is everything all right at home?"

"Absolutely. Everything is almost perfect, no?" Mary smiled, patting my shoulder.

"I think Dilo would be a great candidate for our new after-school anger-management sessions with Ms. Henderson, our sweet, ginger-haired guidance counselor. Have you met Ms. Henderson, Dilo?"

"Screw Ms. Henderson, man."

"Dilo!" Mary smacked my arm. Principal Nixon jotted something on his notepad, while Ms. Lieberman closed her eyes and shook her head disapprovingly.

"I wanna know. Was my thesis clear? Did I present a fair argument, Ms. Lieberman?"

"Your choice of language was unnecessarily shocking and immediately offensive. The vulgarity served no purpose. Find a better word. Be a better writer, Dilo."

I truly believed my English teacher lived with nine cats and slept in a giant litter box.

"But did you get the part about how we're being duped, Ms. Lieberman? How we're intentionally being distracted.

Even all of this. Everything you're saying. This entire school is training us to be robotic monkeys, miss. Don't you understand? You're indoctrinating the youth through education."

"All right, now—" started Principal Nixon.

"My generation is being forced into a great depression, Mr. Nixon. Neither of you are taking this seriously—"

"By what exactly?" asked Ms. Lieberman, smirking like the mean girl she was.

"All that stuff in the magazines, miss. Who do you think controls the media?—"

"I'd be mindful of what you say next, Dilo," growled Ms. Lieberman, leaning forward with her hands on her waist, a scowl on her mug.

"And then there's the movie industry—the whole world's about to change, Ms. Lieberman. We're devolving into full retards with the support of the US government."

"Now, that's enough! There is no place for that word in a decent society!" scolded Principal Nixon, slapping his hand down on his desk. Ms. Lieberman rolled her eyes with her entire neck; I was surprised a ball of earwax didn't drop to the floor.

Mary shook her head in disappointment. Sighing loudly. Looking over at Ms. Lieberman for approval. I heard the birds outside the window squawking behind Mr. Nixon's big empty head. As they talked among themselves, I slid my leg out slowly over to the side on the rug. Tongue on my lip. Full concentration. I dragged the five-dollar bill under my shoe to my chair. I bent over to tie my laces. I rolled my pant leg up. Pulled down the top of my sock and slipped the bill down to my ankle, positioning it so the edges wouldn't scratch my skin.

"Dilo—"

I sat upright.

"Why are there always students congregated at your locker?" asked Ms. Lieberman.

Pew

Pew

She got me.

I was suspended for two weeks plus two days leading to Halloween. More important, I was banned from the school Halloween parties. Don't ask me for any trick-or-treat stories from the year 2000. I got none.

Ms. Lieberman ordered my locker raided, but thankfully I'd sold the rest of my weed before first period. My web use would be monitored until the end of the school year.

"A Confederacy of Retards" would never be read, let alone hit the bestseller list. I lost out on more than just the prize money that day.

My English teacher had a dildo up her ass, and unfortunately I'd never forgive her for it. *"War gets deep, some beef is everlasting."* Some people ride on having "good intentions," when they're the ones who need to learn a lesson or two. Or three. Or four. Whatever.

I had to make up for my losses, in this one life, one life, I had.

Because of my suspension, I was only allowed to leave the house on my own to go to church or Our Meadow, which was a walk and a bit away, not too far from my school. The former, the house of my mother's God. The latter, where I hoped to find mine.

We were in the Purple Prayer Room at Mary's church on Industrial Drive, about an hour and a half's walk from our house. About a thirty-minute bus ride. Mary had been a member for ten years or however long it was we were in the country. Her eyes sparkled when she said anything about the fellowship.

"Is the lipstick supposed to burn?" shrieked a woman. A simple woman. Plain face. Pleasant. Products would actually do her some good.

"That's either the formaldehyde or carmines doing exactly their job, honey. Rest assured, ladies, there isn't any lead in Gary Elle products. This stuff is life-changing."

Anji spoke with her hands. Her fingernails were painted red, grown and shaped to look like she had her life together. A woman worth considering. Her foundation was cakey. Her eyeshadow bright blue. She chewed two blocks of bubblegum from side to side and was unnecessarily obnoxious. Big-blown hair that didn't suit her. Searching for the will to carry on. She was more mascot than salesperson with clumpy mascara and big hoop earrings, and you know what they say? The bigger the hoops, the bigger the fuckup. If my aunty weren't naturally pretty, I swear to God, I don't know how she'd survive. Not a lot else ever worked in her favor.

Seven women sat around the table we'd set up an hour earlier. Cups, compact mirrors, and lotions positioned around plastic rose petals set on a paper tablecloth. Only three dollars remained from the five I'd snatched from Principal Nixon's office. A whole lot of effort went into every "cozy station" for each of our "guests," because that's what Anji meant for me to call them. Even if our setup was fresa-fabulous, the whole Gary Elle job was sloppy from the start.

"Dilo, you've grown. We don't see you at church often. What do you think of this blush?"

"You got higher cheeks than Halle Berry, Melinda. Your husband better watch out."

Melinda was about fifty-seven, with an empty nest and varicose veins. She nearly cried happy tears, overjoyed by the thought of her husband having to worry about the attention her cheekbones could bring.

"Now, if you have a look at the Morning Concealer, all you need is a dime-sized drop. This product is a miracle worker, ladies. One of my favorites. Should slide right on and cover your entire face," said Anji, holding up her hand with a smudge of Cappuccino on the tip of her index finger.

"What if it doesn't slide? Mine doesn't slide," said a woman named Bhanu with a strain in her voice.

"Just mix it with water, honey. Spray your face with

that rose water selection in front of you. With the shimmer cap. That's the one."

Bhanu looked like she'd suffered an acid attack. Instant allergic reaction. Poor thing had her glasses off, so when she looked in the mirror, she was pleased. The women clapped, seeing that Bhanu was happy. Was confident. Was a new woman.

"Gary Elle is about being comfortable in your own skin. Enhancing your beauty with essential-organic chemical products. Your eyes may start to water, but you know what they say: pain is just homeliness fleeing the body."

The women squirted quarter-sized amounts onto their fingers. Product splattered on the flimsy paper tablecloth. Five obedient women followed directions, struggling with the cement we pawned off as foundation. Two other women had moved on to the toner, and without proper instructions it was no wonder they both screamed as soon as the liquid touched their skin.

"That's the Tickle Toner. You gotta laugh it off. Gary Elle puts that on his balls, smooth as two boiled eggs."

And the women laughed. And they obeyed. They had a great time playing with makeup and lotions. Eating the snacks we provided. Some we paid for. Most I had to steal. But I learned that day to never celebrate a win until the trophy's in your hands and you're at home in bed with the prize money.

Anji walked over to Mary and me.

"Brilliant," she said, sliding past Mary to grab a mutton roll off a plate. Something crossed her mind, and she put the roll back.

The ABCs of scamming. Always be cautious. Always be clued in.

The time was five forty-five. Fifteen minutes left to sign on the dotted line and get our money. Fifteen minutes away from two hundred dollars times seven people. That was fourteen hundred dollars, nine hundred seconds away.

"I'm just stepping out for a cigarette," whispered Anji in my ear as seven women filled out forms, cheerful, hopeful, and excited about their own new business plans.

Five minutes passed.

"Where is Anji?" asked Mary in my ear. I shrugged. She handed me a plate of short eats. "Tell her to come, we have no time. Give this to the pastor."

The hall was empty. I could hear a group of teenagers just outside the doors waiting for Youth Worship. They still had ten minutes as well. There were pictures of the pastor, community meetups, campfire summer gatherings held every August for about a week. On this end of the hallway, before the main foyer, there were another two doors for Sunday school.

I smelled Head and Shoulders with a whiff of sandalwood. That was Anji with a hint of tobacco prancing without serious thought, living without realization. Brushing and rubbing her scent on the carpet with her feet. Two doors on the right. Three on the left. The unit was more narrow than wide. The pastor's office was at the end of the hall, opposite the side entrance, which led out to the back parking lot. I had no reason to rush, besides the fact we only had the room for less than a quarter of an hour.

Plus, it wouldn't be so bad to have the women sign on the dotted line in a hurry. I was doing as I was told. The plate of short eats in my hand was for Pastor Childs, and I was also looking for Anji. Out of nowhere, I get this feeling. I want to cry. I want to scream. I want to hide and never be seen again. I want a warm jacket; I want to go to sleep. I'm scared and I don't know why, but it feels like someone is about to hurt me.

I heard a car. I heard a giggle. I heard the slam shut of a door—the beep of the lock—I heard jingling bells, jingling bells, and a moan. The side door opened.

"Oh, what a surprise! You nearly had me falling over. I didn't expect to see Mary's daughter at church, let alone on a Friday."

"Hello, Mrs. Childs. I didn't think you'd be here either."

"I practically live here, dear. Are you ready to attend Youth Worship or are you still devil worshipping and listening to satanic music?"

"I see you're still not a very nice lady—"

"I'm only kidding around with ya, come here, dear—" And she pulled me closer for a hug with her two hands full, holding two aluminum trays that smelled like food from Mona's. The moans in the back grew louder. And then there was a—

"Did you hear that?" the pastor's wife asked me.

I hoped she would've asked about the short eats and how school was. I hoped she would've held my hand, and I'd have steered her to the foyer, to the end of the other half of this horrific hallway.

"I didn't hear anything," I said, but I should've screamed.

I should've stalled. The pastor's wife pushed me to the side and flung the pastor's office door wide open. She dropped her trays, and food crashed to the floor. She covered her face with both hands, and this woman screamed at the top of her lungs before falling to her knees, where she cried beside fallen fish and sticky buns.

Anji had her legs wide open on the pastor's desk, and the pastor was on his knees.

ACT 2

ANJI

OCTOBER 14

In the corner unit of the strip mall across from Z-Mart was my dear friend Mona's diner. You couldn't find a better diner in the city. We met one evening in '91 at the back of my ex-boyfriend Yusuf's van. Yusuf sold imported fruits and vegetables. I gave Mona a deal on her first bag of beans, which she roasted for her signature coffee. Yemeni beans brewed to a bitter chocolate with notes of buttered cherries. She also perfected astonishingly crispy and fluffy donuts that rivaled freshly baked Parisian croissants.

Three people stood ahead of Dilo and me. Theeban Three Scars, because he had three scars on the back of his head. Jumpha Jooni from 12 Silverbell. And Tisha, who seemed to be ordering the whole menu to go. Normally, I never had to wait in the queue, but that day Mona had tunnel vision. I was in the trenches, flagging for her attention. A single glance. That's all I needed. Tables were full. Booths nearly packed. The phone in the kitchen rang incessantly.

I wore my wide-brimmed black hat. My black pleather trench. A pair of kitty-cat sunglasses. Yes, I wore sunglasses in the diner that evening. I wore my sneakers to avoid any unwanted attention.

"They're staring, aren't they?" I asked Dilo, sliding into a booth.

"You're being paranoid," she said, sidling in with the newspaper she'd brought.

She licked her finger and separated each section, folding and piling a stack as her eyes perused headlines. She stopped first at the classifieds, then for the crosswords. Finishing with the jokes and the horoscopes. She pulled out her Discman from her hoodie and placed it on the table. She pressed the play button, which was jammed on one side but fortunately still worked if you pushed the button at the right angle. Dilo pulled her pen out from her coat pocket as I tapped my nails on the table. I fiddled with the salt and pepper shakers. The napkins. I rearranged them so every corner touched. The waiter brought over a cup of black coffee and a chocolate milkshake, and a couple on the other side watched the entire time, whispering to each other. "You better look the other way," I sneered, pulling out my compact from my purse, putting on a coat of my red lipstick.

I saw Mona marching from the front, in my mirror. Her fists tightly squeezed.

"You really thought it was a good idea to come here of all places?" she said, wiping her hands on her apron, shoving herself into the booth beside Dilo. "I would've had you sit in the back if a table was open. Lighting's dimmer on this side, at least."

"What's going on? Something's been said. I can feel it."

"And you have no speculation about what that could be?" she asked, raising her eyebrows, quizzically tilting her head to one side.

"What's there to know, Mona? Why don't you just tell me?"

"People think we're in cahoots," she threw out in exasperation.

"Cahoots?"

"That's what I said. Cahoots. Can you believe it? I've been telling customers—I'm here to offer you great food and beverages. The best you've ever had. Top five in the city—I promise. But don't come in here asking me about no gossip or I'll be cooking your ass in a pressure cooker in just a minute, thanks. Have a nice day."

Mona grabbed her pack of Camels from the front pocket of her apron. She double tapped the box before picking out her death stick. We weren't in the smoking section, but this was her diner, after all. The waiter, Kevin, came over with an ashtray. Mona passed me her pack. The floor was sticky under my sneakers. I felt slightly self-conscious about my hat. The brim was outlandishly wide, and I'm serious, I was never one to want unnecessary attention.

"Hang on. What were people asking you?"

"What *were* they asking me? What *are* they asking me."

"Come on, Mona. Spill it. Terrance saw me put tampons in my purse again? Is that what it was?"

Mona laughed.

"You don't see all those people peering in the window?" she asked, smug and cool.

"There's one child looking in right now. Just one—"

"The pastor at Industrial Drive has a wife, ya know?" I laughed this time. My word. I laughed and took my time doing so. I took off my sunglasses and sat back against the booth. I enjoyed that cigarette. It was the last taste of peace I'd have for a while.

"Someone asked if I was trying to stall the pastor's wife yesterday, because I told her to wait an extra ten minutes when she was here to pick up sticky buns and fish rolls for their six o'clock prayers. We had corn bread coming out the oven and all I wanted was to give Rebecca a fresh loaf. On the house. Something nice for God's people. But you can't be too kind these days."

"What were you stalling the pastor's wife for?"

I wiped a drop of coffee I'd spilled on the table with the tip of my finger. Mona looked over at Dilo from the sides of her eyes.

"She can't hear you. She's busy. She's got her headphones on."

"She doesn't want nothing to eat?"

"She's fine, Mona. Please. What are people saying?"

Mona put her hands on the table.

"They're saying you gave the pastor a blow job, Anji."

"I beg your pardon?"

"You heard what I said."

"I gave *him* a blow job?"

Mona kicked my shins under the table. I flung my head back, and I laughed even harder.

"*He* was the one on his knees!"

"He what?!"

"You heard me!"

"All right, hang on—"

"Now, you listen to me, Mona. I was at the church for a business meeting. This close to closing deals. Anyone mention that at all?"

"You were at church for a revival, is what I heard—"

"I was fifteen minutes away from closing a fifteen-hundred-dollar deal. Clients were happy. I only wanted a smoke. You know how it is. Two minutes of peace to myself was all I wanted, but then—"

"You saw Miguel?"

"He was in his office. Hair gelled back. Khakis. Green polo. I could smell him from down the hall—he practically called me over."

"He called you over?"

"You remember—"

"I used to help y'all pass letters."

"So, you can imagine the tension between us, Mona. And a decade brewing. His face. His eyes. And, Mona, he shut the door."

"He shut the door?"

"Immediately."

"What did he say?"

"Said he was sorry. Said he found out his mother was sick that night and that was the beginning of the end for her."

"He couldn't call?"

"I moved houses, remember? Moved from that room to a basement before moving here."

"He could've asked any of our friends for your new number. He could've done a lot more than nothing."

I shrugged. Ashed my cigarette. Sipped my coffee.

"You knew he was married."

"I wasn't really sure."

"Oh, Anji, stop."

"I was ovulating, Mona. I hadn't been touched in months. I was wet from the moment I smelled him. Blame chemistry! If my senses have gone out the window, that's my biology. His pheromones all but pushed me toward his desk—"

"Anji. You know I don't agree with any of this. Sometimes you get carried away—"

"He kissed me, Mona. He pushed over a Bible. Summer camp flyers fell to the ground, and before I knew any better, we were kissing and kissing. And then—"

"You stopped? You came to your senses and stop—"

"He lifts me up."

"He carried you?"

"Up to his desk."

"What were you wearing?"

"A short skirt and a blazer. A lace camisole underneath."

"So, he has you on the desk? Give us a minute, Kevin. This is getting good."

“His hands run up my legs. Under my skirt. He gets on his knees. Pulls me closer to the edge of his desk. His grip, Mona. He kisses my thighs. His lips caress my skin, and his tongue—”

“You sure she can’t hear us?” Mona pointed to Dilo.

“She’s fine. Are you listening?”

“I have a customer now. You gotta get to the point, dear.”

“I was so close, and he says, *If I look at you any longer*— so I held his head, sliding my fingers through his curly hair— You remember his hair, don’t you? Well, the door opens just as my body arches—an entire cosmos bursts, splashing colors on the wall—”

“Good grief. And my sticky buns?”

“All over the carpet, Mona. The pastor’s wife screams. Poor thing. She lost her mind, of course she would. My heart dropped to my stomach. And when Pastor Childs stood up to console her, his khakis—soiled. Wet . . . The pastor’s wife—”

“Rebecca.”

“Rebecca faints on the carpet, Mona. People ran over from the hallway, from the foyer, thinking she’s dead. That I shot her.”

“My God.”

“Miguel played a huge part in all of this, but apparently, I was the one on my knees? Those monsters.”

Mona’s hands covered her face. Elbows on the table. Her staff took care of the customers strolling in. Eventually, she regained her composure. She adjusted her apron and fixed her hair.

"All right. Listen," she started, stern, and how I needed her. "People are watching. People are talking. You know how it is around here. The both of you should've been less impulsive, but I get it. Just . . . be cautious right now. You know how people get when they hear stories about kinky women. Now, do me a favor and get your asses out of here, and don't come back until this all calms down."

She held my hand and blew me a kiss from across the booth. She slid out and waddled back to the kitchen, asking one of the chefs to give Dilo and me a ride home.

For all the things to say about that Friday evening, I will say this very true thing. I didn't know Pastor Childs was married. And even if I did, so what; I was the one in control.

MARY

That horrible feeling. That horrible pain. You could see my cortisol rising through our bloody roof from down the street. En theivamey! My own church shunned me. They threw my belongings out the door. My bag. My muffins. All the Gary Elle crab. They threw out our boxes. All right, they placed each outside nicely, but my God, nobody even offered us a ride. Thankfully, Tracey, who had been minding Maysha, lent us her car that Friday, but none of them knew that was the case. Nobody said, I'm so sorry this terrible misfortune has happened to you. Nobody said, I'm sorry we can't have you remain in our fellowship because your sister is a vesi, is a slut. No! They threw me out like a dog to the curb with my wayward kin and a daughter who told the church people to burn in hell and die!

I still want to vomit when I think of that terrible evening. *Chi!* Embarrassment is worse than death.

But the Lord hath said, trust in Him with all of your heart, and do not lean on your own understanding.

OCTOBER 19

The Tamil Radio played from my dresser. A drama about the King of Snakes. A giant multicolored serpent worshipped by the gentry as the laborers waited outside the gates.

My sweat soaked the sheets. My body was completely motionless. I thought maybe I could manipulate my toes with my mind. Move a tiny inch. With all my might I tried. But nothing. I lay on my bed.

In Jesus's name. In Jesus's name.

I had the most peculiar feeling that I was going to die. This is the day that the Lord hath made and I will be dead by night. My body sunk to the coils in the mattress.

In Jesus's name. In Jesus's name.

My metamorphosis begins in my head before my muscles start to ache. Before my scales form and my skin hardens. My body pulled as it kneaded itself internally, as my bones snapped and each rounded end formed and shifted itself into a new order, as I stretched into my new skin. For He prepares a table for me in front of my enemies. Anointed, He fills my cup.

Ssst
Ssst
Ssst

Maysha ran into my room and jumped on my bed. She crawled on my stomach and shouted.

"Periyammaaa!! I want a fuh-king snack!"

In Jesus's name. In Jesus's name.

I flicked the girl's lips and slithered to put some clothes on before getting her ready to go outside.

Terrance. That fat man. He stood by the door of the Z-Mart entrance as Maysha and I walked by. He didn't smile. Word must've gone around, and I felt a thousand eyes on me.

It was You're-in-Luck Thursday at Z-Mart. The floor was open to solicitors. Open to businesses to distribute cards, discuss vision, sign up customers for many sales. Plus, 15 percent off ticketed items on the store floor before the next week's new bargains.

I wore my jacket. The very special jacket I'd made for myself some years ago. I stitched an eighteen-inch pocket on the inner lining. A few compartments in the sleeves and practical pockets on the inside with double lining. I put Maysha in her puffy blue coat, secure in her stroller, with a small distraction. A pack of gummies made with real fruit juice and 60 percent sugar, guaranteed to keep children on their best behavior.

The aisles were far too crowded. The floor was packed

with salesmen and saleswomen holding out their business cards. Z-Mart workers in their red vests and shirts, and solicitors wearing blue badges. Dilo had called this mayhem. "An infestation of human fleas." Of course, seeing there was no room to even squeeze, Maysha wanted to walk. She pulled her safety belt. She pushed the button, shouting. She climbed from her stroller, almost toppling to the ground. Aiyo! That child was a pain. I grabbed her hand, knowing this could be how I lost her.

Snack. Bologna. Toothpaste.

In Jesus's name. In Jesus's name, keep us from watchful eyes.

"Excuse me, ma'am, would you like to try Krafty Kon Cheese Strings? Only two ninety-nine," said a Z-Mart worker in red.

I shooed her away as Maysha held out her hand for cheese.

"I'm part of a government-funded project where we help unemployed folks upgrade their résumés," a young man said as he held out a blue business card.

Maysha took one card. She collected them all.

"You look like you love the environment. Do you have a second to chat? We're looking for people to help join our human chain to stop the construction of a Walmart on pine and cedar territory just off the 401."

"Have you tried the Tier 4 nails for the Nail Gun Pro 2000?"

A hand flew in my face. Then a nail. Really, that fool almost jammed the bloody thing in my eye. I grabbed Maysha quickly. The solicitors moved closer. Their hands. Their cards. That patronizing tone in their voices.

"What a cute baby. I'm Lisa, a Krafty Kon Baby Beauty Scout. Are you interested in changing the world with your daughter's smile?"

Through a small stretch of people, we were almost as close as we could be to Pantry Goods for a snack. Very close, I could see boxes of Teddy Grahams and tea biscuits. And just when I thought we'd found peace with a small box of animal crackers in my hand, a man called from behind me. He ran over, panting. Really. Believe me. A light shone around him, and not just because there were table lamps on display beside him. He was a handsome man, so I wasn't so alarmed to see him. He held out his sturdy hand and I offered mine in return, seeing he had a golden cross around his neck. Glory to Jesus.

"My dear sister, the Lord wants me to tell you something. He sees your tears, sister. Are you ready for a new home in the Lord?"

The man held out a white invitation card.

The Way of Truth Evangelical Church. Where sinners are welcome. In Jesus's name, I cried.

DILO

My appa wrote me letters. I could recognize his handwriting upside down and squinting. All the curves and angles. The slant in his "I." I kept every stamp in an old Polly Pocket. My letters in a shoebox under my bed. He wrote once that Mary gave me all the crazy I'd ever need to be famous. He said funny stuff like that.

This is what I've said to you at least every month since you were born.

The most important concept to understand is that of "symbiosis."

Be wary of parasites around you.

Happy 12th Birthday, Dilo.

Mary said the man never knew what to say or when to say it. That he was socially inept. She called him a "brainless donkey." She asked if he ever wrote that he loved me. She said that he should stop writing me notes altogether. Send some money instead. He sent me plants he pressed between cards. Shed snakeskin. A pretty pebble or whatever.

This is "gneiss," pronounced "nice." This, speckled iron. Here is a porous chunk of basalt.

Mary said my appa was the cheapest man she'd ever met.

My appa left Jaffna two years after we did, in '92. Mary said he sent us packing. But he just wanted us to be safe, he told me. Safe in the cold of the world, far away from him. He applied for scholarships in Europe. Said he'd meet us later. Could get a higher degree or a job, or whatever.

My appa wrote once that he had a moringa tree he grew in a greenhouse. A greenhouse he had in his backyard, in a new country, on his new property, where he required a visa to live legally. He wrote about his squash. How it trailed and climbed up to eight feet high along his shed and up an oak tree. He wrote how the aroma of his garden after a heavy rain was his second-favorite smell, only after the scent of my head when I was a baby.

My appa had cool stories, I guess. Or he wrote them out, so I would remember. He tracked sloth bears, dissected capybara pellets. He went on a two-page rant about Nestlé and the IMF. About dairy farmers taking their lives. The horrors sparked from milk powder. Back Home was number one in selling tea and committing suicide. That's what he said.

My appa stopped writing when I was thirteen. Who knows what Mary told him. So, I remember the few letters he sent me.

The bus crash round a hairpin road in '59. He'd never been so happy to be alive. Hanging from out a window at the back of the bus. An accident, he stressed. But not when the Sri Lankan army arrived. Lined up all the people along the side of the road. Got the men butt naked. Old Man Shiva was a retired economics professor who lived down our lane. The army beat him to the ground. Instead of crying "aney" when they hit him, he screamed, "Aiyo, en theivamey."

My appa was a Jaffna man, so he knew all kinds. Or he thought he did, and was very inclined to share every one of his opinions, is what Mary said. Especially after a little hot toddy on a Sunday with his ink pens. Mary worried the airmail was monitored. That his letters would spark alarm. Public enemy number one. Menace to society. The police would come for my arrest. I wasn't allowed to repeat what my appa said. Not ever.

The last time I heard my parents on the phone, Mary put the speaker on.

"Don't stop reminding her of her first five years. How we ran. How we hid in bunkers. How the shelling never made her cry. How well she sat still during explosions."

"Leave it, Kannan. There's no place on earth you can't get shot and die. We're here now, and we're happy."

. . .

Whatever.

My appa had a wife and kids in Germany. I think his kids were half Chinese. Some kids had interesting mothers. Some kids had present dads. None of it bothered me.

OCTOBER 20

There were no more tangerines in the fruit bowl. There were no mangoes, no pawpaw, no butter fruit. No koyyakka, no sugarcane, no mangosteen. The fruit bowl was empty. There was not a fruit or a vegetable in our entire house, not even some Mary could have picked off a tree in the neighborhood.

"I'm telling you, vesikal, just listen to me for once!"

Anji, Maysha, and I looked up at Mary on the kitchen counter. Gray jogging pants hoisted above her waist. Socks on her feet that were perfect for sliding, and a wooden spoon in her hand. Somewhere down the timeline of Mary's life, something terrible must've happened to her at least twice. Then maybe another few times, because how was anyone that out of their mind? I couldn't tell ya. She never disclosed much to me about her childhood besides how she caught frogs after the rain stopped, opposite the Batticaloa Lagoon, when she was seven.

With the kitchen chair against the cupboard, I knew Mary was happy with herself for managing to get up that high on the counter without falling on her ass. I saw the flash of shock register when one of her feet slipped and she realized her choice of socks could be the death of her.

"I'm talking to you, vesikal! Why don't you dogs ever listen? Do you want to burn in hell for eternity?"

"For fucksakes. *Wheel of Fortune*'s on! They're about to solve a puzzle." Anji slapped the back of my head.

"Watch your mouth," she sneered.

Mary had the spoon in the air, before pointing toward the three of us. She looked like a Speakers' Corner drunk on a Friday night in the cool of October.

"Do you know how grateful you should be in this Christian country? Would you prefer to be raped and killed and then raped and killed again?"

"Jesus Christ, Mary. Should we think about getting you some Prozac now?" asked Anji, studying the ends of her hair for splits and damage.

"Quiet, you sinner! You be quiet now!"

"I need a cigarette."

Anji opened the utility drawer by the kitchen phone for her tobacco tin.

"Do you think a bomb wouldn't have dropped on your heads? Do you know how blessed we are that Kuta Maama sponsored us? Thank the Lord for His mercy. Thank God we didn't arrive on an illegal boat."

"What's your point, man. The commercials are on. Hurry."

My head out the doorway to the living room eyeing the TV, Mary took ages, and I didn't want her to fall.

"I could be taking drugs in the bus shelter, gambling in casinos. Drinking in the park. Having boyfriends. Sleeping in their beds. I could be holding hands in the street and touching men much taller than me. Buying expensive bags. Using someone else's money. But no! I found purpose in my Lord."

"If you had a boyfriend . . ."

Anji couldn't help herself. She had a rollie in her mouth, still managing to sneer, still fumbling through the drawer.

"Shut your mouth, vesi. Do you know what people say about you as soon as your kundi leaves the room?"

"You better hold your tongue, akka, before I drag you off the counter."

Anji still rummaged through the drawer.

"When was the last time you fed your daughter with your hands?"

"Where's my lighter?"

"If I fall, my Lord will catch me. But what about you, vesikal? Do you think people think you're beautiful? You think they want to hear what you have to say? You think you stand a chance in their world? You think so? Even with all that blush and foundation, you're still just their island trash. You're all the holes in your body. You'll be used and abused before you earn a single dime, or a teaspoon of respect. Don't you ever talk to *me* as if I'm nothing. I'm a child of the living God and He has spoken to me. We *must* go to church and repent."

We left Mary to her monologue. Whatever the hell that was. Anji finally found a lighter and lit her rollie in the kitchen. My head was in the fridge as I opened a pickle jar. Mary whipped the wooden spoon at the wall.

Honk
Honk
Honk

There was a commotion coming from outside. A song playing on max. Shania Twain on a Friday night on *our* block? Kinda unheard of. Maysha raced to the front door, and the subwoofers did nothing for the mediocre bass. Anji held Mary's hand as she stepped down onto the chair leaning against the kitchen cupboard. She held Mary's hand as she stepped off the chair and onto the floor again.

It was about 7:20 and the sun was done for the day. The streetlights were on, and Monty Dame drove by in her pink Caddy, ten miles an hour, cruising. "That Don't Impress Me Much" played from her car stereo.

"What's the matter with you?"

Anji walked up toward the road where Maysha was, smiling and waving at Monty. Monty's nails were fuchsia. Her hair was permed with blond streaks. She had a pizza box on the dash, and I wondered who she was attempting to lure out this time.

"Oh, come on, honey! Our block needs a little excitement. You can't be the only one having all the fun."

Monty winked at Anji. I thought her false lashes would slip off. She was making money, and with her money she'd grown a pair of balls.

"You playing that off a CD?" I asked.

"Columbia House, sugar. CD two in a box of '97 classics."

Aside from Shania on blast it was a quiet night. Everyone seemed to be settled in and cozy, but then from around the bend of our block came a second pair of lights flooding the streets. Another pink Caddy honking. Another woman waved from the driver's seat. Fresh-cut bob. Nails professionally filed. Melinda. The woman from the church with the blush, and her cheeks were flushed with that pink stuff. She smiled with a new set of veneers. Chiclets beaming in the dark. Melinda was remade in Monty Dame's image and it only took seven days.

"All right, gotta skedaddle. See you honeys around," Monty said, winking. "Oh, and, Anji, keep working those contacts, sweetie, don't lose faith now." Then she carried on with her parade, driving ten miles an hour, Melinda trailing behind her.

The four of us watched the lucky winners have the time of their lives until the Caddys were out of sight. The music became faint, and then all you could hear was the owls and crickets again. Mary was the first to head back to the house. Anji had Maysha in her arms. I was picking at the white cedar bush on our lawn looking for leaf miners, when Mary turned round. Her brows scowling, her lips pursed. Here was a woman pissed off.

"You're all coming to church with me this Sunday or you'll find me dead in my bed in the afternoon. You hear me? This family needs God."

She slipped off her shoes in the foyer and put on her house slippers. She walked down the hall to her room and shut the door.

Dearest Dilo,

It was '87. You were two years young and your cheeks were plump; your face was as round as a tomato.

It was '87. We were at Shiva maama's house a few houses down. His daughters were abroad studying. His wife must've been in Lebanon then. One afternoon Shiva maama made odiyal kool, which of course your mother didn't eat. She claimed she saw him pick his kundi before emulsifying the tamarind in the coconut head.

It was '87. The Indian Peacekeepers were on patrol. It had only been a week since the Jaffna Hospital Massacre. They killed babies. They raped girls. They shot and fired on the spot. Foolishly, we left you alone at home with the servant girl. Her name was Thangamani.

It was '87. Shiva maama had a cigarette. I admired the sky. Cerulean. The color and the word remind me. Ceylon. Ceylon. The way my mother once said it.

It was '87 and a crow flew into Shiva maama's pawpaw tree. It cawed and cawed. There was a stillness before there was a rustle. A cobra slithered by my feet.

It was '87, and your mother and I ran down our dusty lane. We ran and we ran. Looking back, we floated.

It was '87 and you were crouched on the side of the road three houses from our own watching ants carry blades of turmeric leaves up a palmyra tree. Your mother grabbed one of your arms, I grabbed the other. We ran to our house together, where the front door was left wide open. Shut and locked. I pushed a table against the door. We ran to the back of our house. To our bunker.

It was '87 and a tank rolled by, crushing bones to sand.

Ra-ta-ta-ta

Ra-ta-ta-ta

Dishoom

Dishoom

I have a daughter, Dilo. She is your half sister. Her name is Thangamani the Second Returned. Two weeks ago, we went to Disney World. She was most pleased.

OCTOBER 22

You ever wonder where your money came from? A single coin or a single dollar. All the nasty stuff on the metal, on the paper. All the rips, tears, and germs. The codes and doodles some of us scribbled, messages to the bill's next keeper. Would they appreciate the gesture? How sacred was our dollar in their hands? How bad did they need that paper? Would they ever pass that dollar on to the next owner without putting up a fight? And would that next person be me?

The Way of Truth Evangelical Church had the softest carpet. This was Big Daddy's house, all right, and I wondered what the mortgage cost. Stepping through the wooden doors into a sold-out concert, praise and worship booming loud on surround sound.

Whoosh
Whoosh
Whoosh

"At the cross. At the cross. Where I first saw the light. And the burdens of my heart rolled away."

Two screens, one on either side of the effervescent stage, the holy man altar. That early afternoon, as was the case every Sunday, the pews were jammed, bodies side by side, all the way from the main floor to the canopy. Worshippers were on their feet raising their hands in praise, dancing in the aisle, Crip-walking their way as close to the front as possible.

Only those invited could speak on the mic, blessed with the opportunity to share their message with the great multitudes. On the stage was a grand band, with seven separate percussionists. They backed a choir in burgundy robes with wide-open mouths, surrounded by the finest calla lilies, smelling of floral rain.

Weaving throughout this lavish production was a camera crew, violating personal space for a money shot. Eyes rolling back. Tears down a druggy's face. A single mom with thinly drawn eyebrows and a nose ring, speaking in tongues, and a man—a strong, decent man—in a clean, crisp shirt, surrendering to the Lord with a smile on his face. This church prayed for a pay-per-view deal every other Friday. A Jimmy Swaggart–esque fever dream, with an American flag tucked in the corner way off in the back, where no one would see. A Star of David displayed prominently on the pulpit.

Pastor Todd Mackenzie didn't look like a man Anji would want to hug and hold, or whatever, so that was a good sign. He was a stocky man who exclusively wore three-piece suits. He marched in front of the pulpit with a Bible in his chubby cherub hands. When Pastor Todd spoke, he dragged his syllables along verses and made songs out of psalms. The man knew how to perform. He was a snake charmer, or whatever.

"'And the Lord said to Abraham.' Genesis chapter twelve.

'I will make you into a great nation,
and I will bless you;
I will make your name great,
and you will be a blessing.

I will bless those who bless you,
and whoever curses you I will curse;
and all peoples on earth
will be blessed through you.'

"Glory hallelujah. If you're saved by the blood of the Lamb, God's promise to Abraham and his people is also a promise to you. Church, do you hear me? For we his people will fill the Land of Canaan. From the river to the sea.

"Let the church say, 'Amen and amen.'"

I knew where five dollars in one of the golden plates passed around the pews came from. The five I tossed in, that was half of what remained from my emergency dental surgery funds. I was supposed to buy milk from the convenience store after service. But I'd been feeling really funny. I couldn't tell if it was my conscience or my acid reflux. Burping out air. Hoping I wouldn't throw up.

"Your guilt is a blessing from the Lord. Your conscience is a holy policeman. Give and seek His mercy, and you will not be judged by your sin, for the Lord is the only giver of peace everlasting. John 16:33. 'In the world ye shall have tribulation; but be of good cheer.'"

I surrendered the five dollars I had in my pocket to God, after the pastor dropped that. For sure, there was something in the air. Maybe even a gas leak.

What the Way of Truth Evangelical Church had over

other churches I'd been to, besides being next-level eerie, was the spectacle they made out of the testimonies. It was *prime time* up at the altar. Thou shalt not covet those who have the spotlight, indeed. Approximately fifteen minutes were allotted every Sunday for members to give accounts of the blessings and wonders of God. Those who had been healed, those who had been promoted, or those who had made some extra dough. Those who no longer fantasized about extramarital intercourse, people no longer filing for divorce. I swear I heard a woman say, and I quote, "Praise the lord, my daughter had an ectopic pregnancy. She won't be a teenage mother, no more, no more, no more."

After the testimonies that Sunday, the pastor called for those in need of salvation to come up to the altar. Without a thought, Anji stood and made her way. She had no other choice with the promise she made to her sister. Plus, Mary was sitting right beside her. Of course, Anji still tutted and huffed and puffed, but I knew Anji had her own scheme. Anji operated with intention. Anji wanted to be seen.

We didn't hustle because we enjoyed that ache in our ankles. We didn't con because we got a kick out of playing tricks and fooling people. Trust me, if there was another way out, we would gladly have taken it. To be honest and "good" and half-decent were privileges we weren't afforded. To survive in this world, if you were poor or hurting or saw through the rain of bullshit, required a warrior mentality, and then to play the damn game—

Anji was a lot of things, but my aunty wasn't stupid. My aunty was no coward.

In her most modest black dress, showing not a single curve, she stepped up to the stage when the pastor called her. Her face was broadcast on the big screen.

"The Lord says, you are a woman in need of His mercy. What is your name, sister?"

Anji's lips parted. She closed her eyes.

"My name is Anji, and I was a whore, and a whore I want to be no more. I need a miracle. I need an opportunity."

Her voice strained.

The pastor closed his eyes. He moaned and he hummed his own melody. He stomped in his spot on the red carpet, on the stage, by the pulpit. The gold chain across his suit pocket caught the spotlights, and the screen twinkled. The fat in his cheeks jiggled. He placed a hand on Anji's shoulder.

"In Jesus's mighty name. The Lord has a message for you, dear Angel. From the book of Genesis 2:18—'It is not good for man to be alone. I will make a helper suitable for him.' Glory to God, sister. The Lord will find a man for you. He knows just what you need. Only if you believe and surrender to our Lord and King will you know life again."

Pastor Todd Mackenzie put a fat hand with all his golden rings on my aunty's head and said, "By the grace of God, sister, you are saved."

Anji's knees buckled. She fell on her back, hands in the air, slain in the Spirit of whatever the heck that was, shaking in fits, trembling on the carpet, out of control—anointed by the power of desperation. The congregation praised their Lord.

We made it through the pastor's performance, we made it through Anji's. Mary and I were surprised to see that among the few in the front pews was Sheila, the woman I set up at Z-Mart, the woman who thought she was too good for a pat-down. There she was in a forest-green pantsuit and pink heels. Showing off her fresh pedicure. Her baby. Her kid. Her husband in a navy suit with a forty-two-inch chest. Wannabe catalog family. Standing around at the front of the sanctuary right after the service. Smiling. Creepy.

"Do you remember me? Sister Sheila. Sister Sheila. Do you remember me? Four sixty-four Jarvis Street. I was the cleaner for six years."

"Oh, my goodness. Of course. Hello, sister. Praise the Lord."

Mary, Mary, full of grace, blushing cherry red. She shook Sister Sheila's hand.

"Please. Please. Take my number. Come to our house after service one day. I will make for you *verry* nice food."

Mary hit my arm. I gave her the pen I had in my coat pocket. She wrote our home number on the back of the slip of paper Sheila handed her. A Body Shop receipt.

I lost out on five dollars that day because of unwarranted guilt. We could be homeless in a couple months, but there I was supporting my mother like a good Christian kid. Devoted daughter. Keeping my opinions to myself. Giving my mother a little less than what she hoped for.

ANJI

At the back of the church, down a small hill and onto a level patch of grass, there was a weeping willow tree. The ground was soft from the rain the night before. I lit the smoke in my mouth. Every second, releasing. Releasing. Losing my bite. Breathing. My left hand feeling light. My fingers shaking in front of me. Heart still beating faster than usual. Jesus Christ. God's covenant with Abraham? I exhaled and tried to regain my composure.

"I'm surprised anyone made it down here," said a man, smiling, as he walked over.

"There's a path just over there." I pointed.

"I don't mind getting a little dirty. You got a lighter?" he asked.

Tall and "dark," meaning olive. I couldn't place the man's migration. His skin gave little away. He wore a Hilfiger shirt, Dickies slacks, and Timberland boots. Three sprays of Paco Rabanne. His clothes were baggy. His style familiar.

I rolled the spark wheel, lighting the cigarette hanging from his lips while on my tiptoes. My chest brushed his leather jacket. Cowhide and Dippity-Do, a comforting freshness. The warmth of his breath was enough to lure me into fantasies far from any good for me, followed by the seductive scent of lingering tobacco. I looked up into his eyes.

That Sunday the leaves were as warm as they were at autumn's peak. Reds. Golds. Rusting into brown. I could feel the man looking over at me. Wondering when to speak.

"The Holy Ghost really got you in there."

"Ha. He sure did."

"The pastor called me Doubting Thomas when I first went up to the altar."

"Is that so?"

It was chilly. I put my free hand in my pocket, the lining in my cheetah-print coat doing the job of keeping me warm, in October.

"I lived a different life. Let me tell ya. You know what I used to do on Sunday mornings?"

"Please . . . ," I said, blowing smoke from my lips, hating myself for smoking. My fourth of the day.

"I opened my mouth too soon. I do that sometimes. Just blurting shit out—"

The man made the sign of the cross.

"Well, I'm curious now."

"Curious about what?" he asked.

A blank look on his face. The thought must've slipped away.

"About what you did on Sundays before the Lord saved you, what do you think I'm curious about?"

"All right, calm down. I know the Lord's saving isn't a quick fix. I got a lot on my mind, all right? So, you said you were a whore. Up there on the altar, you let a lot out."

"Praise the Lord, I'm saved."

"Glory to God. You're saved."

He half smiled.

"So? What was it? What did you do on Sunday mornings before coming up to the altar and asking for God?"

". . . I was hungover. Saturday nights I hung around Benny's watching girls shake their tits onstage. Strippers, I'm talking. *Whores.* Some of those girls put their asses right up on your face like that's what they thought you wanted. *I just wanna window gaze and enjoy my cold beverage, lady. Take it easy up there,* that's what I'd tell them."

He inhaled. I exhaled. Together we fell into a rhythm. Loud synchronized breaths, in and out, in and out.

". . . Have we met before?" he asked.

"I don't think so."

"Well, praise the Lord. He saved a roach like me, He'll save a roach like you. It was nice meeting you."

He flicked his cigarette toward the willow tree and headed back up the hill toward the church.

DILO

I've had stalkers before. In real life, I'm talking. Ask any girl in our area how many men followed them home in their cars after school. Trust me. They called me Uncle Cusser on these streets. The amount of uncles I've verbally assaulted. The number of dads. It didn't matter if it was raining cats and dogs with fleas or if it was minus twenty-two degrees, if any of those bozos ever asked if I wanted a ride, the answer was always no. Universal Rule Number 1: don't be stupid.

I met a guy named A.J. once who followed me every Tuesday and Thursday after school. True story. I was heading to Our Meadow for air, for answers, to kill some time, the following Tuesday.

"Why aren't you in school?" he asked that afternoon, leering from his open window. His tongue pressed against his top lip. He had this look on his face, all smug and beady-eyed. Made me want to slap him.

"You don't got any other business to mind?" I asked, screwing up my face in disgust. Raising an eyebrow. Hoping he felt nothing but shame talking to a kid almost half his age.

"You're looking at one of Dino's Biscuit Factory's stars. Packaging manager, honey. I have plenty to mind, thank you very much." He laughed, shaking his head in disbelief. "You can't win being disrespectful, thangachchi."

I gave A.J. Mary's number. The rest is history. You make things work for yourself when you can. You ask the right bozo if you must. You take what you can get your hands on, even if from a stranger.

OCTOBER 27

A whole shelf of peppermint and it wasn't even the first week of November. What a bunch of yahoos. What a bunch of dunces. What a bunch of . . . well, I'm not allowed to say that word anymore, am I even allowed to think it? As if this would save us from what was to come. Inevitable disaster. Every December a small distraction. Boom. Jesus of Nazareth was born. Spend the money you have. Spend the money you don't. How about a Krafty Kon Peppermint Pie? Peppermint Chocolate Ribbon Cookies? Red, white, and green fluff to stuff up your butt while you roast a damn turkey. Fifty percent off ducks on Christmas Eve. That was our tradition. Cheapest poultry on the shelf. Exotic enough. Whatever. Halloween wasn't even over, and Mariah Carey was singing her Christmas tits off. People weren't safe anymore. They preferred to be whatever the heck this was.

I fiddled with a wooden train set displayed on the shelf below. Short enough for most children. Raised the hand of the wooden conductor, signaling the train was ready. *All aboard!* Pleasant-faced wooden people celebrating Christmas way too early. A white dog with a spot round his eye had a goofy smile with his tongue hanging out. I put him in my pocket for Maysha. I liked to give her things when she behaved.

Wrapped in a winter coat and scarf, a boy stood messing around with the display on the other end of the shelf. I sidled up beside him. Wasn't even that cold but he was bundled up tight. He undid his zipper. Had these cute orange woolly mitts clipped to the ends of his sleeves. The boy, who was probably four, didn't care about the train set. The Krafty Kon Kristmas Koyote was what he wanted, like every other kid on every other block, because of the newest commercial. Unfortunately for him, the Kristmas Koyote was sold out. Four days before November.

"Psst. Hey, kid."

The boy looked up. Strands of his hair stuck to his forehead. Real sweaty. He had round glasses that made his eyes look magnified. Bifocals, was it? He was a cute kid, is what I'm saying.

"Thirty bucks, what a rip-off. Not including taxes. Cost five dollars to make. Never mind the Chinese kid who made 'em. But fear not, little boy. I got Koyote. Best price on the market. Ten bucks. Just for you. Whaddya say? You got ten dollars? Your parents around?"

The boy yanked his hat off. That's when I noticed his hearing aids. I felt like a jackass. I also hadn't noticed the man standing on the other side of a box of peppermint pretzels, looking over at me and the kid. Loss Prevention at Z-Mart store 416 was a joke.

"What's going on?"

Anji was at the end of the aisle with the buggy. Maysha sat in the seat for once, strapped in and behaving.

"I was looking for you," I lied.

Anji noticed the boy but said nothing. I walked over and threw a carton of peppermint cakes into the cart, knowing we'd ditch them later. Potential Loss Prevention still loitered by the Christmas shelf, rubbernecking as if I didn't clock his dumbass.

"I wanna see the Santas," slurred Maysha, pointing toward the Christmas shelf with a limp arm. Kid was drooling. Her eyes rolled back. Her head was about to fall to her shoulder like a drunk's on the bus from Kennedy Station late at night.

"You gave her cough syrup?" I whispered.

I raised Maysha's delicate eye folds as her eyes closed, watching her pupils kinda hang like dark brown Christmas decorations.

"I gave her a little more than usual by accident. Do you have what you need?"

"In my pockets. Pads and cheese in my bag. Detergent, but the smaller box—"

"That's fine."

"You got yours?"

"Plus a little extra. We should leave the buggy somewhere—maybe Pantry. And our ruse, Dilo. You're sure the musician comes in—"

"Every week since they stopped giving lunch vouchers on Thursday. He'll be here."

Anji and I scanned the area. Kids occupied Toys. Potential Loss Prevention onto another teenager in a hoodie. Right when Anji was about to lift Maysha up from the buggy, so I could push it off somewhere unexpected, Mary, gleeful and clueless in her yellow jogging set and clear plastic raincoat, waddled up to us with a full basket.

"Praise the Lord. All this Krafty Kon is only two ninety-nine."

She struggled to lift the basket into the cart.

Anji examined the contents. Peanut butter, fish sticks, breakfast waffles. A kid across from us ate a bag of pickle-flavored chips, licking his fingers, as his mother pushed their shopping cart full of stuff to make a kid happy.

"We have a list, akka. We only have twenty dollars."

"Only twenty? I thought you had some overdraft."

"Overdraft? I used that for my boxes."

"That Gary Elle crab? I thought some man gave you money."

"Some man? Which man? Who would give me that much money? I'd love to know what actually runs through your mind—"

"Hang on a second. Hang on—" I interrupted.

I held Mary's hood. The one on her *clear* plastic raincoat. Clear as in transparent. That woman had lost her mind.

"Why the hell are you wearing this jacket? Why aren't you wearing your other jacket?"

"You saw the rain. What do you expect? Walk here and catch a cold?"

"You didn't hear anything we went over this morning? Everything we said. Did you not understand where we were going? What the fuck? We talked about this."

"Don't talk to me with those words, naaye. I am your mother."

Mary was up in my face looking ugly. Anji slapped the back of my head.

I sorted through the items myself. We didn't need cream cheese. We didn't need chocolate wafer cookies. Or blueberry muffins with caramel pieces and a brown sugar topping. Or Christmas bread with green crust and red sesame seeds. Sure, bomb stuff that's all that and a bag of chips, who could resist—but we had to make difficult choices.

"I pray a thousand prayers, and this child wants me to bother God about a cold I caught from the rain? You have some money, no?"

Her face. The look on her face. How could I even describe it? Unflinching. This woman. Five foot three with strands of gray coming through. This woman who'd done no harm in her entire life but birth me, asking if I got money to give her for food? I was down five hundred potential dollars from the essay contest, plus the loss of income due to my suspension. I was not going to let this woman make me lose my cool at Z-Mart. Not on the front line. The fox recognizes traps. The lion frightens the wolves. Classic Machiavelli.

I saw a man with white church shoes, blue trousers, and a black shirt walking toward us. As I predicted, Tommy Two Tunes with his pants hanging real low, a sweatshirt chewed up by moths under a pink jacket, strolled over with a banjo slung around his back. He took his stance in the middle of the toy section on top of a striped red beanbag, just as he had the week before.

If I worked Loss Prevention or security, the whole area would be manned in preparation for Tommy Two Tunes's weekly concerts. People had patterns. Routines. There was order in chaos if you understood it.

"Good morning, ya mental degenerates! Who wants to hear a song about crack cocaine?"

Tommy Two Tunes strummed and strummed his heart out. A string snapped. His pants were four shimmies from falling to the ground, and a Z-Mart worker ran over from the Lego aisle.

"Sir. Excuse me, sir. Sir? Hello?"

A Filipina, four foot eleven, in a red Z-Mart vest hurried over. Tommy Two Tunes howled and hollered about lighting up a pipe to the tune of "Hot Cross Buns" as they tried to force him down off the beanbag.

A group of children gathered round him, eyes wide, in awe of the spectacle. All of which was unnecessary. An inability to identify problems. The result of so much failure. A lack of organization and strategy. A clown show every step of the way.

Finally, the undercover Loss Prevention agent strides over from Pantry Goods telling everyone *there's nothing to see here*. Terrance marches from his front post with a megaphone in his hands, turning on the siren, and it's blaring. If there was a time to run, it was just then, just as I'd predicted.

We had two minutes. Less than.

Anji was unsure. Anji had been slipping for weeks. Even before the Gary Elle fiasco, something had been up with that woman, but of course she'd never say. She'd suddenly started spending a lot more time at home and was less involved in our petty scheming.

"Should we take the basket? Just walk out with the basket?"

"How do you expect us to run outta here with a basket? This is our branch. If it was downtown, maybe, but we can't go running out of our local shop with a basket. What the hell is the matter with you?" I asked her, with genuine concern for her mental health.

"Wait, wait. I need an umbrella. I'll go and grab one," said Mary, ready to venture off into mayhem again.

The priority was to bounce—scram the hell out of there—and my head was a millimeter away from popping. We had a plan. A perfect plan, and now my aunty, and my mother, and my cousin-sister, drugged and sleeping, were pissing on the entire operation. The doors were clear of security, for the moment. But they'd be checking those cameras like hawks that night.

The apple may not fall far from the tree, but what if the

apple was taken across oceans from where it first grew from a seed? Would that apple rot?

Before I gathered my last nerve, about to walk out with whatever I had up my sleeves, the man with the shiny white shoes, blue trousers, and black dress shirt tapped Mary's shoulder from behind. Mary smiled as soon as she saw him. Her face even glowed a little.

What did I think of the guy? My first impression: Who wears white dress shoes unless they're a disco dancer? He looked like he'd never been in a fight before, and you couldn't ever trust those kinds of people. The guy was kinda normal looking, I guess. Kinda cute. He looked like someone's annoying older brother.

"Glory to God," he said, with a slight upturn of his lips. A smirk or a grin or whatever. His expression changed when he saw Anji, though. I couldn't tell you how. Before I could figure it out, he caught me staring. I looked the other way. He handed Mary and Anji his business card. He licked his lips, and I don't know why he did that. His lips were smothered in Vaseline.

"Lucky me for bumping into the both of you." He smiled; his canines sparkled. He had distinct teeth. Like a serpent. A carnivore. A creature that bites. Enigmatic. That's the word. He was enigmatic, I guess.

"Praise the Lord. My friend who introduced me to our new church," gushed Mary.

Anji was coy. Anji feigned cool.

"Looking beautiful. The both of you. I hope you don't mind what I'm about to say. I know you're independent women. But I feel the spirit of the Lord moving through me. Can I buy these groceries for you today? Can I pay for your shopping?"

Mary gripped the man's hand with both of her hands.

"Glory to God. Brother, what is your name?"

"Mark. His name is Mark," read Anji from his card.

Was I suspicious of the guy? I was suspicious of everyone, but not everyone offers you a dollar. Who wouldn't accept free groceries? That didn't seem so bad. That didn't seem so bad to me at all. The way I saw it, we just had to keep our guard up, and my guard was high. Twelve CN Towers high. Free food? I wasn't worried.

MARY

My sister had her problems. One look at her and you'd know, ha, that woman was trouble. She was a complex character, no? An intellectual turned whore. Besides the fact she was a karuppi, meaning a *verry* dark woman, something had happened to her, long ago, and she was never the same. One day, my sister didn't come home, and we wouldn't see her for eight days. On the evening she returned, aiyo en Yesuvey, she walked into the house like a pey. She was filthy. And her clothes, my God.

Dirt crammed under each of her fingernails, some of them broken, some of her cuticles bruised. One of her pant legs was shorter than the other. Blood had dried on her neck and on her cheek; flecks of mud and tiny scratches riddled her skin. Oh Jesus! She carried a horrible scent that filled the house and still hangs in my nose insufferably from time to time. *Chi!* She's never said where she had been, or what had happened, but people don't take suffering lightly. I am no one to speak of politics, but we are all people, no? And like our Old Man Shiva used to say, the political was personal. *Chi.* Leave it. What can I say?

My sister was a Tiger. A resistance fighter. My Lord, all that we lived before age thirty-three. The world in which my daughter was born. *Chi.* We were half of ourselves. Maybe made a quarter. But by the grace of the Lord, we could be made whole again.

OCTOBER 28

It was a glorious Saturday the Lord had made and the honey-colored leaves were the most splendid. Proverbs, chapter 3, verse 5. "Trust in the Lord with all of your heart, and do not lean on your own understanding." It had been almost a week since our first visit to the Way of Truth Evangelical Church, and believe me—I had been on my knees crying for His mercy. The one who knows how many hairs are on my head is the one who will lead and guide me. I didn't know how we would find our way. I didn't know when the windows of heaven would open for my humble family, but I obeyed my Lord. I trusted my Heavenly Father, who speaks when I call Him.

Two days. Two days of steadfast prayers and fasting since Anji's salvation, since sin was cleansed from our home, and the Lord had answered on that Tuesday, when the phone rang ten minutes after eleven at night. A man named A.J. said to me, Hello? Miss Mary? I have a job for you. Please, let me hire you at Dino's Biscuit Factory. Please, come join our team.

My Lord Jesus. Just like that. All of the devils I had rebuked, all the tears I cried for that miracle. I had a joy unspeakable, it was full of glory. But of course, with blessings comes more testing. I needed $200 to start my new position—for the jackets, and aprons, and gloves. The steel-toe boots, hairnets, and trousers. My uniform, no? I didn't have that money, or any idea how I would manage. But again, I had faith in my Lord.

When Mark handed me his business card at Z-Mart that Friday, I knew he was sent by God. His business card read: *Mark John—here to make you money. Acts 5:39.*

Direct perfection. I called him right away and explained my situation. Without any hesitation, he said we should celebrate, so I suggested Mona's Diner. I didn't care for that woman, and I don't think she was fond of me. But I had to admit she made some *verry* heavenly treats. She brought us a pot of coffee and gingersnaps "on the house." Meaning for free. Mark ordered for Dilo and me, carefully making selections. I brought Dilo along with me because that useless girl was still suspended from school, and having seen her moping, watching more films than reading, I thought a Saturday outing would do her some good. *Chi.* They even banned her from the library! What could we do with our children except keep them by our side?

Mark was *verry* well dressed in a denim shirt and trousers. He had his laptop open on the table. His BlackBerry Rim pager, *another* pager, and an Ericsson phone, too. That man had a Bluetooth, you know? He said you couldn't find one on the market, but he knew a *verry* important person in Hong Kong who owed him some money. That's what Mark told me. He seemed to have it all.

Dilo had her headphones on, listening to her music too loud for her own well-being. That girl will be deaf by forty. You wait and see. She had her schoolwork with her, and I was pleased about that, at least. She was *verry* studious when she had to be; praise God she didn't need glasses from all the books that child read. A pair of specs were almost $250. My child did need braces, though. She also needed threading. Her eyebrows and mustache. Her entire face, her arms. My God. Children were *verry* expensive, especially in this country.

All of those treatments were costly, and doctors didn't marry ugly girls. Dilo would be *verry* pretty if we sorted those matters for her. Only, we can't have our girls looking their best or how will they finish school without getting kidnapped, or worse? A mother had much to worry about.

Sometimes, I was grateful we had less. Who would we be if we had a little more? Have you met people with savings? Ha! I'm laughing. The Lord said in 1 Timothy, the love of money is the root of all evil. You cannot serve two masters, no?

We were at the table. Mark held my hand sitting across

from me. He had dimples and softness in his eyes. He was a sweet fellow. He was charming. He was *verry* good to me.

"Congratulations on your new job offer. Candy boxer, is it?"

"Snack packager," said Dilo before increasing the volume on her Discman.

"Yes, and I told you, Mark. But I need two hundred dollars for the jackets and aprons, you know?"

I wanted to laugh. Really, I wanted to laugh. The way my voice came out from my mouth. High-pitched and squeaky. Who was this man holding my hand and how come it felt so cozy? I kept my face as sincere as possible. I was glad, you know? I was glad. Mark was like a brother to me. He told me I was the big sister he'd never had.

"Well, how 'bout this . . ."

He slid an envelope across the table, all the while still smiling. The music from Dilo's headphones lowered in volume beside me. She turned her head and attention toward us as I slid my finger across the envelope flap.

"This is two hundred dollars," I said after I'd counted.

"And it's yours."

"It's mine?"

"What for?" asked Dilo, taking the money from my hand.

"Pay me back when you get paid your first paycheck. In two weeks or whenever. It's no big deal. Come on. Don't make a scene. Give me two twenty back, if that makes you feel better. Let's call it interest, what do you think?"

Mark's dimples were a gift from God. He reached for

my hands again. Ha. I was a schoolgirl. I was revived with a hope I had feared I lost at the parking lot on Industrial Drive, but Dilo studied Mark closely. Her stare nearly set Mark on fire. There was a brief pause of silence at our table, and for a second, I began to worry.

"Deal," she finally said.

She handed me back the bills. We shook hands in agreement. Mark pulled out a strawberry sweet from his pocket.

"These help when I'm craving a cigarette." He grinned, sucking the candy in his mouth.

I hadn't formally introduced Mark and Dilo. We didn't do those things. If you spent time with my family, you would come to know us. Simple. Otherwise, nothing was forced. Our business was ours, including our children. But Mark made an effort with my family. Before Dilo put her headphones back on and returned to her schoolwork, Mark pulled something out from his jacket. Some wires wrapped around a small gray square.

"You ever hear an MP3 before?"

He passed the gadget across the table.

A quick flash of my daughter's crooked teeth. For whatever reason, her smile was a rare sighting. She was different that way. She held the foreign object in her hands, unsure, but still with a glimmer in her eye. An expression of excitement I hadn't noticed before. She untangled the wires. The headphones. She put a bud snug into each ear.

"There are three albums on there. Twenty-seven songs. It can hold about thirty. Starts with *The Slim Shady LP.*"

Many of Dilo's first experiences were taken from me. I

couldn't enjoy having a baby, even if I didn't know what to do with the girl. We were always running. You can't sit still during shelling. You don't notice first words, first steps, first tantrums. War was absolute. Every person you've ever known could be taken from this earth in a second, and you wonder about those people firing bullets. What did they think they were fighting for? What about my child? What about the children we heard crying in the distance, hiding in cupboards, singing sweet songs, singing sweetly.

With the earbuds in her ears and a bass sounding from her bubble, the hair on my child's arms rose. Really. Instinctively, she closed her eyes. A new state of being, my God! I worried this was the devil's music player, but Dilo's smile brought Mark a satisfaction he couldn't hide.

"All right, that's enough," I said. "Give it back to him now."

I pulled an earbud from Dilo's ear.

"I have another one. You get gifts at these trading conventions. It's yours, kid. All yours. Don't even think about it."

Dilo put the other bud in my ear.

"Stick nine-inch nails into my eyelids? My goodness! In Jesus's name." I flung that bud out from my ear. Dilo and Mark laughed.

"Change the song or I will take the bloody thing. That music isn't good for children!"

"She's a Tamil kid from Malvern, that's nothing," Mark said, winking.

"Would you say like this if you had those nails inside

your eyeballs? Aiyo, I can't even think it. *Chi!* That music isn't godly."

Mark laughed. He squeezed my hand. "I'm teasing you, Mary. That's not even a song I downloaded. Your mom's right, kid. Forget about that album." He pointed his finger sternly at Dilo. The girl rolled her eyes and increased the volume on the player, returning to her bubble.

"My sister," started Mark, most sincere. "I'm sorry you had to hear that."

"No problem, my dear. Only God knows what that child listens to. But you listen, Mark. I am actually here for some real business." And I pointed my finger at him this time. He was pleased. He turned his laptop around so I could see the screen. Two graphs were in constant movement. The bustling market, he called it. My God, it was something to behold.

"It only takes two days—"

"Two days?"

"Well, no more than three, with God's mercy."

Mark opened a notebook he kept in his bag. He pulled out a small whiteboard too. I didn't understand much of what that man ever said to me, but I trusted the creator of the universe.

"But if I don't have any money?"

"You have nothing of any value to sell?"

God had led us to Mark, or how was he sat in front of me? Was the money he had put in my hands real? Yes. Absolutely. That was the only answer I needed. The Lord's faithfulness was my shield.

Mark drove us home in his Ford Escort. He drove fast

at times. Riding over speed bumps. But there was a cross hanging from his rearview mirror. Along the edges of the car mats were crumbs. In the cup holders, large paper cups half full of flat cream soda. In the back, a briefcase, a gym bag. Brown paper fast-food bags scattered on the ground. He was a busy man. A bachelor. Tracey had been minding Maysha, while Anji distributed résumés at the Eaton Centre. After we picked up Maysha kutti, I invited Mark inside our home, though he was happy to wait in the car for me. He sat on our couch. Maysha put the TV on to that shopping channel. Dilo went straight to her room.

"I will be one minute, okay? Sure you don't want a tea?"

"We just drank a whole pot. You take your time," he said, crossing his legs, sitting comfortably. Flashing those dimples of his.

My suitcase was pushed further under the bed. I had a few appliances in boxes. Gifts people had given over the years. A rice cooker. A kettle. Pot of Gold chocolates that were missing. I knew Dilo had had her hands under here.

"Dilo! Dilo! Maysha!" I called.

Maysha ran to my room immediately.

"Go get the broomstick, kutti. Go get it and come."

She dragged the broom through the hallway and threw it toward the bed as I crouched, still trying to reach the suitcase handle.

"Is there chocolate?" she asked.

"Not now, kutti, please," I scolded, getting closer to moving the suitcase with the broom, shifting its position slowly.

Finally, I snapped the buckles open and unzipped around. That smell. Documents. Certificates. My silk Kanchipuram sari. My father's hanky wrapping my gold. I had a side pocket with some smaller pieces. I pulled out a thin bracelet—thin but still worth a few hundred.

"The little cutie says there are chocolates in here."

Mark was at the doorway. I shut my suitcase and pushed it under the bed quickly, my heart pounding, my blood pressure rising. I stood and saw Mark smiling. His dimples, no? He held the Tamil Bible I had on the coffee table. Maysha hid behind his legs.

"Oh no. No chocolate here. Please, at least let me make you a sandwich before you leave," I said, leading him to the kitchen, shutting the door behind me.

ANJI

OCTOBER 30

Mark invited me to a restaurant, *downtown.* Said he was a shareholder, so wine was $4.99 a bottle. Hardly any lighting, zero seating. Minimalist and industrial. Guests stood at high tables covered with long checkered tablecloths. Affordability under the cloak of contemporary style.

A woman walked in from the brisk night with a baby on her hip. She walked from table to table before arriving at ours. She was young. Her hair mousy brown. Thin and greasy. Fingernails bitten down. Her child looked about a year younger than Maysha.

"You got five dollars, sir? My kid needs some diapers is all."

"I got five dollars and a message from Christ, all right? Jesus says go home, it's getting late. You're way too young to be wandering round begging with your baby on ya. Get it together, kid."

Mark handed the girl ten dollars before turning his

attention back to his laptop, studying every incremental movement of the graphs.

I noticed the women in the restaurant. A brunette, a blonde, a Black woman, and an Indian. Average-looking men seated opposite these gorgeous beings. Men paying for a woman's time in some way or another. Women batting eyelids. Only ever smiling without showing their teeth. The young brunette wiped her mouth with her napkin. The man triple-checked his pager. The brunette wore a tight red minidress. She was tall and thin. She walked to the restroom with her chin up, showing off her *perfect* profile, her plump lips, her teeny tiny nose. Beauty sculpted by the hands of her technician, her surgeon, her god. Confidence with a price tag.

I arched my back. I maintained good posture. I ran my fingers through my ironed hair, flowing down my back. I pulled my top down. My bosom hoisted in my bra, my breasts only a third as spectacular as they were in my twenties, yet still wonderfully fabulous, and mine. Ogled by babies. Babies and chimps.

"Ya know, you look at a kid, and you know they think they're ugly. They think so without a shadow of a doubt, but it doesn't bother them. They're too smart to care. They got a hobby already. No point worrying about the face they've got. They find interests, ya know. They're so smart, they figure that out early. You gotta have interests."

I thought of my ex-lover, as was the case when I was ever with another man.

"There is no one like you. Still. There is no one. Please don't judge me."

I slid my hand over to Mark's as he reached for a bread stick. He pulled back and nervously smiled.

"It is a little chilly. That young mother left the front door open," I said, resting my head on my clasped hands with my elbows on the table.

"Shut the door," shouted Mark.

The hostess at the front looked over her shoulder.

"What kind of boyfriend are you?" I blurted. "I mean, do you treat your women right?"

"Oh." He laughed. "Look up 'terrible boyfriend' in the dictionary, and you'll see my face with two missing teeth or something." Mark made a silly face, crossing his eyes and sticking his tongue out. He was one of those men who was debonair so long as he kept his mouth shut. His tongue was white, he had many fillings. He said ridiculous things. I knew I could never kiss the man and enjoy it.

"Is it that funny?" I asked, half smiling.

"I'm thinking of my ex. She sprinkled hamster shit on my bed one night."

He made the sign of the cross.

"She needed to be tranquilized and she's lucky I didn't do it."

"Well, I'm here to support you. As your friend," I said, rubbing Mark's arm.

The woman in the red dress walked back from the restroom. I knew she was there. Everyone in the room did.

She was behind me. In Mark's eyeline. From his laptop, he looked up at me, until he looked up at her.

"Hey," he started, with a solemn expression. "If a girl comes by with a baby asking for five bucks, tell her to go home, all right? She might listen to someone like you, about her age."

"Sure." The woman blushed. She put her head down and carried on to her table.

"God, the look on her face."

Mark squirmed. His expression. Disgusted. Appalled. He clenched his jaw. He looked over his shoulder at the couple, sneering. I ran my fingers through my hair. I pursed my lips. My mission was simple.

"So, these are the graphs . . . ," I said, pointing to Mark's screen.

"Took some time, but now I'm feeling pretty fly. Couldn't afford the training. Costs five grand, ya know? Glory to God in heaven. I should be getting a Beamer soon."

I dragged my finger along the crook of Mark's nose.

"You buy low and sell high?" I asked, pulling his earlobe.

"I'm sensitive," he said, blushing and brushing my hand away.

He opened an Excel spreadsheet.

1000–1400
500–800
2300–2455

"Last three trades I made for one of my guys. Leon."

I wasn't an Excel expert at the time, but I had some familiarity with the program from when I worked in data entry at the insurance company. There were other tabs. Other tables. Other groups of investors, possibly. Other accounts? It was evident there was an increase with each return. At least, from what I saw on the screen. The first trade was made on August 10 of that summer, and the most recent was a couple days prior to Mark and me standing for dinner. *Downtown.* I took a sip of my wine.

"You're a busy man."

"If you have my time, consider yourself lucky."

His eyes still on his screen, on the graphs, he snapped his fingers toward the hostess.

"They should have toothpicks on the table," he mumbled.

The hostess noticed Mark but turned the other way, dragging her finger down the reservation list. Picking up the phone.

"Is there a problem?" I asked Mark, pointing at his screen again.

"There could be a problem but there doesn't have to be. The entire job is risky—"

"Are you making as much money as you possibly can?"

"That's a little personal. The question's a little personal, don't you think?"

"Oh, I apologize. I meant, I'm here to help. If you need me."

I smiled without revealing my teeth, with just enough

comfort in my eyes. I twirled my glass and took another few sips, giving Mark the space he needed.

He held his glass of water before deciding to have some wine. He licked his lips and wiped his mouth with the back of his hand, his attention still directed to his screen.

"I usually have traders sign waivers, ya know. Some people tell ya they'll invest, but they're too chicken. They don't have faith, they don't trust God. They don't hear Him speaking. They need the Almighty to bash their doors down with signs and cymbals."

"But if there was a sense of urgency? The elections are next week. I heard the results could stress the market. Is that true? Do you have a plan? Oh, what am I saying? I'm out of my depth here. Do you still feel cold? It's still quite chilly inside." I was mindful not to scare him away.

Mark pulled a cigarette from his pocket. He lit his smoke and blew from the side of his mouth, adjusting his shirt collar.

"You always know what to say," he said, flicking ash into the tray on the table.

"What do you mean?"

"You always know what to say. Like you're reading off a script or something."

"I beg your pardon?"

"Are you a fed?"

"Am I a federal agent? Are you serious?"

"Just be yourself around me," he said.

"I am. I am being myself—"

"I'm tired enough working people all day, so just do us

both a favor, all right," he said, still engrossed with the graphs. I inched a little closer and put my arm around Mark. I massaged his shoulder. His body was stiff.

"Hey. Hey. Relax. We're having a great time together. I'm having a great time with you," I reassured him. He didn't even bother to look up.

DILO

NOVEMBER 2

Maysha was in the living room watching the shopping channel, toys scattered; you'd think there was a party of kids that just walked out. The ponytail we'd managed to tie with Maysha's short hair stood up like a firecracker on her head. She had a clump of Vaseline on one side of her head. She wore her *Caillou*-themed pajamas. Jelly? Was it jam? Purple stuff all smeared and dried on her back. Unfazed, Maysha sat cross-legged on the carpet with a plate of chicken nuggets on her lap. Chicken nuggets that I had not stolen for her. No one had. And we had no money, so I knew nobody bought 'em. Not a dollar under the couch. Not a dime under the bed. We'd already devoured most of the treasures in our home.

But in the kitchen that day our fridge was full. Our freezer too. And on the counter was an abundance of tropical and regional fruit in the bowl, in piles, in rows, in net bags, in boxes. Never in my entire life had I smelled that sweet of an aroma from my mother's kitchen, and my ma's kitchen smelled pretty good for the most part. But that afternoon—if I had a machine to bottle that smell I could probably sell it for $95 at a Whole Foods.

While Maysha watched TV, eating her nuggets, we were in the kitchen. Anji, Mary, and I. Anji pinned Mary with her back against the mustard-yellow wall behind the kitchen table, opposite the painting of Jesus on the Mount of Olives. One hand round Mary's neck. The other with the letter opener at Mary's jugular. The sisters were eye to eye, practically growling. I'm surprised Mary's tongue didn't spill out and whip Anji across the face. I was hunched over the sink trying to catch my breath.

"Listen closely, akka."

"Go ahead, vesi."

"Where did all of this fruit come from?"

"What fruit? What fruit are you talking about?"

"The whole cornucopia on the counter, you clown," I shouted, this close to throwing a Fiji apple from behind my back at Mary's head.

"I don't understand your English, naaye. Anji, what did Dilo say? Anji, please. Corn-a-what? There's no corn on the counter, you fool."

"Jesus, Mary. There's about eighty dollars' worth of fruit up here. We're not going to argue about the existence of the fruit. They're on display like we're at a bloody market."

"And praise the Lord for His blessings."

Mary raised a hand and closed her eyes. You could tell she was damn well proud of herself for something.

“There are rambutan. Two pomegranates. A box of mangoes,” I listed.

Mary waved her raised hand and smiled.

I turned back toward the sink, hunched over.

“I’m going to ask you one more time, akka.”

Anji tightened her grip round Mary’s neck, and I knew because of the sounds Mary made. That croaking. The cutting off of air.

“Mommyyy!”

Maysha walked to the entrance of the kitchen from the living room, scratching her ass with one hand, scratching her head with the other. A pajama pant leg rolled up on her ashy leg. A side of her pants hanging low. Potbelly out. Crumbs on her face.

The second that child got to the doorway, Anji’s hand dropped from Mary’s neck. Letter opener on the table. I turned back to face the tiny human with the goofiest mug I could offer. Mary rubbed her neck. Coughing. Heading toward the sink.

“Mommy, they got a gumball machine on the shopping channel. I think I want it, Mommy. I want it, Mommy. I want it real bad, Mommy. Pleeease.”

“You need to stop watching the shopping channel. Let me feed you some dinner.”

Anji pushed me aside with her hip to reach the fridge.

“She had nuggets,” Mary said to Anji, filling the kettle with water.

She looked over at me, hunched in the corner.

“Sit and eat. You look like you’re about to drop dead. People will think we don’t feed you children. Look at how skinny your face is. Your eyes are dragging down to your chin. Lord knows if one of you has jaundice. Aiyo kadavuley!"

Mary handed me a bowl of rambutan.

We were at the kitchen table. The three of us. Maysha was forced to watch the news in the living room with a bowl of Froot Loops, the only fruit she'd eat if it wasn't smothered in condensed milk or in a bowl with ice cream. I bit the skin of a rambutan and sucked the juice before pulling back the roughage.

Mary peeled white fibers from a segment of tangerine. Her fingers always looked tired to me. She took a breath and gazed up at the picture of Jesus holding an orb of light across from her.

"I started a business."

"You started a what?" asked Anji, wiping her mouth.

"A business. I, too, am a businesswoman now."

There was a spiderweb on the light above the table. A jumping spider trailed round the rim of the fixture as my chest did that thing it was doing. That thing it did when air in my throat got all stuck and I couldn't set a single breath free.

"What do you mean you're a businesswoman? What the hell are you talking about?" asked Anji.

"My business partner said, no matter what, I am guaranteed a gain of ten percent. Minimum ten percent of what I give I will be granted. I couldn't even believe it. We prayed together, too."

"Just a minute. Who said this to you?" I asked.

"My business partner. That fellow. That very nice fellow, the boy who paid for our shopping at Z-Mart. The one I owe two-twenty to. You were there, you goose."

"How much did you give him? Who do you owe two hundred and twenty dollars to?"

Anji was gobsmacked. She was out of the loop, unsure of what to make of the information presented to her, and with my aunty, she's gotta know the score.

"Take it easy, Anji. This is my business. It's consequential—"

"Confidential."

"Con—whatever. My business is my concern."

"I need a cigarette . . ." was all she could muster.

"Both of you need Jesus, is what you both need."

"You didn't spend that two hundred, right? That's for your work gear," I said.

"Do I look like a stupid?" asked Mary, tutting and kissing her teeth, smiling at her newfound superiority. She dipped a fig biscuit into her tea, satisfied that peace had been restored.

"You sold your thaali. Is that how you got the money?" asked Anji.

"Are you crazy?"

"So, a bracelet, then? You sold one of your two bracelets."

"*Chi.* Leave it, Anji. Please."

"Where did you get the money to invest? Why do you owe this man money? Akka. What are you not telling me?"

Mary laughed and shook her head.

"I would never sell my thaali. I sold Dilo's gold bracelet. Don't give yourself heart palpitations. Please."

"I had a gold bracelet?"

"Not now, Dilo!" Mary snapped, pointing her damn finger at me. "Mark had said the elections could make the market uneasy. I didn't have time to think . . . Praise the Lord, look at what we're eating."

The air stuck in my chest, or was it the lack of air in my lungs? A doctor had ruled out asthma when I was in the seventh grade and asked me if I was ever anxious. I smiled and asked, *About what?*

The jumping spider still hung on to the rim of the light fixture, and the American news was loud from the living room. God knows what the Tamil Radio dragged on about. All I remember was Mary's dry lips, mouthing the words, with crumbs of fig biscuit on her tongue. Tiny little seeds. Miracles in her mouth.

"Mark is coming to our home with his investors. He will show everyone what he is doing."

"He can't do this at his house?" I blurted.

"His house is under renovations. He's staying with a friend in a small basement. Don't be rude, Dilo."

"We don't even know this guy."

"He is giving us a computer."

"A what?" I asked.

"We're connecting to the World Wide Web. Money will be made under this roof. Can you believe it?"

I wouldn't know all the details. Nobody ever would. Even at the very end, we never really knew.

I bit into a rambutan. I peeled back the curly spikes and poked my fingers in, pulling apart the skin. On the glazed, moist flesh, a worm looked up at me. I put it in my mouth.

Our Meadow was a scrap of grassland, a parking lot, sheets of lawn, and a COMING THIS SUMMER sign. No way was it anywhere close to what it had been five years ago. Back then, you could find insects in the tall grass. I'd seen a hummingbird once round the columbine, cicadas and crickets, and bees on all the wild bergamots. Milkweeds tall and wide. Then I saw it all disappearing. We were left with newly built town houses, narrow and cramped. Stepford assimilation. Not even human, just made-up make-believe. Rosebank Gate, Magpie Manor, and Glenshower Hill in construction on the east side, blocking all the morning sun from our beloved field. The tall grass and prairie blossoms, and all the insects fucking. The wild things that made all this living better. Much better than this.

ACT 3

MAYSHA

Every visit walking down the street to Z-Mart for a treat, there's an original new item to view. And Maysha thinks, *Hey! What a wonderful thing for sale. That I can learn to work and play. And get, if I cry loud enough to my mother.*

Maysha stood in electronics all by herself in front of a pink television set blaring loudly. On the screen was a little girl with JonBenét hair in a highchair, eating two scoops of ice cream from a bowl. Beside her were three bears in rocking chairs, slurping from cones with different flavors.

"Mmm! Bubblegum! And it's jussst right! Krafty Kon Bubble Kream. A million dreams in a single bite!" said the girl, smiling gracefully, working the camera. Delighted by the taste on her spoon.

Maysha caught her own reflection on a blank TV screen. Her hair was short. Tied in a straggly pony that sat on her head like a pineapple top. She looked up at a woman in a red Z-Mart vest. Dozens of buttons dotted both sides. All different colors, all different sizes. Employment recognition for only the best. A piggy with a blue bow tie—most enthusiastic salesperson on the floor. A cash sign with wings—most coupons handed out in a single shift.

"Krafty Kon Bubble Kream. Did you want to try some, young lady?" asked the worker.

Maysha nodded eagerly, noticing the woman didn't have any ice cream with her. She had a booklet of paper instead.

"Here's a dollar off a tub from a Z-Mart in Richmond Hill, darling."

She ripped a brightly colored coupon from the booklet and handed it to Maysha.

"Maysha! Maysha! What the heck, man!" called Dilo from outside Electronics. "We don't have time for this," she huffed.

Maysha smiled at the woman and waved, running over to her cousin-sister, with the coupon held proudly in her hand.

"Excuse me. Excuse me," called a woman with a blue badge. "You have a very cute baby. Is that your daughter? I'm Lisa. Krafty Kon Baby Beauty Scout."

"We're not interested, lady," said Dilo, dragging Maysha behind her, as Maysha held out her hand for the card, waving goodbye to the woman, smiling like the girl with the JonBenét hair. Friends with three bears. Maysha imagining a bowl of bubblegum ice cream.

DILO

Was I ever worried about the internet? A lot of people were. Plugging into cyberspace from public places, from the library or school, wasn't like plugging in from the privacy of your own room. Even if the whole house shared a computer. This was personal. Sitting in the dark, dialed up and connected, felt like living on the edge. Username and password. Make it tricky, but not so much that you forget. Something silly. Something real. A date of birth. A year. Littlefreckledbuttcheek67.

If you were going to be on the internet, alone and without supervision, which was becoming the norm, you needed thick skin. Rubbery and inflammable. Quick wit and common sense or you risked losing your identity. Your savings. Your email chains. If you didn't forward messages to the right amount of people, you risked dropping dead. Or so the message read. You had to be cautious online.

People could find you. Stalk you. Kill you. Chop you

up in pieces. Stories were all over the news. Personal accounts on the web.

Multiple women reported missing after man (43) posed as Bengal cat breeder

Mark came over with a brand-new Intel desktop. A hundred twenty-eight megabytes of ram, eight gigabytes of hard drive space. Windows 98 on MS-DOS—I mean, we had the cream of the crop, apparently. The cherry on top wasn't the fluffy red pompom with googly eyes he stuck on the monitor, but the ease with which I could cruise into cyberspace from the comfort of *my bedroom.* Ain't no other sound as soothing as that scratchy static signal. Ain't no other feeling like sitting in the cool glow that filled my room when the ceiling light was switched off and the sun was long gone. The house was asleep, and I was pulled into a vortex—Cowboy Galaxy—a place for gunslingers and trolls. Cry babies and whores—people wanting an escape from reality. The space to be free. A home for the brave. A fountain of knowledge and lies.

Mark took care of the installation. He downloaded applications and set us all up with our own user accounts. He even sorted out emails and gave us all a tutorial. We had games. Britannica bookmarked, just for me. We were officially plugged in to the New World.

I wasn't worried about the internet. But it was big. *Real* big. So big I naïvely believed that if the internet wasn't real it couldn't harm me.

John Gotti –

Hustle Baby? Cool name

Hustle Baby –

John Gotti is pretty sick too

a/s/l?

John Gotti –

23/m/New Jersey

U?

Hustle Baby –

18/f/The Confederacy of Turds

John Gotti –

LOL

Hustle Baby –

Do you know how to block messages and file shares?

John Gotti –

Ur Virus Scan isn't working?

Hustle Baby –

Should be

Can people still send me viruses?

John Gotti –

It's possible they can ruin ur life

U gotta b careful online

Wanna play checkers HB?

ANJI

When life is quiet, enjoy it. Enjoy it as much as you can. The tiny and the simple. Standing outside on a brisk November night—the perfect cliché—the stars are as bright as they'll ever be. Your slippers are snug. Your robe keeps you cozy. You have dates and cashews in a bowl inside. Black tea in a mug between your hands. You reflect on how well you've managed through the day. *What a glorious evening,* you think. What could possibly hurt you, considering all you've lived? And then the clouds start spitting and a drop falls on your chin, on your hands, and before you can react it's pouring. Never mind. You have dry clothes in your closet. A functioning heater. And you love the pitter-patter as the drops hit the ground.

NOVEMBER 3

I had written out the Rules for the Internet, printed and taped beside the monitor on a large neon card, using a THICK black marker. I told every person who sat in our new office chair at our computer table, *more than once,* to read the damn thing. The rules stated: *Don't talk to strangers. Don't talk to strange men. Don't talk to people you don't know. Tell them nothing about yourself.*

There were nine of us in Dilo's room encircling our computer like it was a god. Never mind the laser printer. Never mind all the paper. There was a portal on the screen. The market, the graphs. The scrolling stock exchange. Mark had his laptop open on the computer table beside our monitor. Two screens glaring the trading platform Global Freeze.

The room was small. We were late to pay our gas bill, but with the heat generated among the nine of us and the running computer, the house was made warm, and our guests were none the wiser.

No one had seen Mark work his "blessing," as we called it, but of course we were curious. What did this man do to generate *at least* 10 percent on every investment? How did he make profits appear as if on demand? What were the first things we'd buy if he was able to keep this momentum?

Mark introduced us to a group of his investors that we called "the Original Batch." There was Leon. A butcher, five foot six and pudgy. Much too young to be a silver fox but the gray suited him well. He was a husky man with an eagle tattoo on his forearm, a half-naked woman on his biceps. Her legs dangled from under his T-shirt sleeve. A faded pair of terribly drawn clogs on her feet. Four months prior, Leon had lost three of his fingers slicing a cut of rib eye on the job at Sugar Maple Barn, a meat packaging plant and a subsidiary of Krafty Kon Limited. Leon was a hardworking family man. He supported his mother, wife, and two kids, who'd arrived from Sarajevo in '92. Leon had given eight of his years to Sugar Maple Barn. You'd think they'd care about his misfortune. But they fired Leon for a safety breach instead. Employees had already complained about faulty machinery, long hours, and being underpaid. Poor guy wasn't a member of any union and, like many, wouldn't risk the threats of deportation. Sugar Maple Barn argued that Leon should've worn gloves while operating heavy machinery, and that the fact he didn't was evidence of *"unforgivable negligence on the part of the employee."* Leon ought to be appreciative the accident had resulted in the dismembering of only *his* fingers and not another staff member's. Leon had entrusted his entire life savings to Mark, is what I heard rumored.

Leon sat on a red stool in our semicircle around the computer table, tapping his chin with his finger stumps. Beside him, hunched over in a folding chair, was Reina with a pink notebook on her lap. Recently divorced and living in her '91 Caprice station wagon. Her children had thrown her out of the house with no explanation and stolen half of her savings. No one asked Reina for any clarification, and she never mentioned much. She was a peculiar woman. Quite shy and petite. She'd giggle and play with her hair, sometimes covering her face while looking away if you stared in her direction too long. She was a lovely woman, don't get me wrong, just a bit off. Well, Reina eventually received a small settlement from life insurance. She met Mark "just in time" as she left Christy's House Women's Shelter, where she'd sought refuge. Mark volunteered there every other Thursday. One auspicious afternoon, Mark ran into Reina in the parking lot. "You don't look so happy. Have you heard of the one called Christ?"

He invited Reina to the Way of Truth Evangelical Church, believing this was God's plan. How did she begin investing? She said that, as soon as Mark uttered his very first word to her, she felt overcome by the Holy Ghost. Mark felt the same. How much did Reina hand over? She never shared that information with me. But her returns were enough to keep her happy. Without gossiping too much, I believed that Reina thought she had a chance with Mark. He made her blush and giggle. Reina once told some of the Original Batch, and Mary, that Mark had gifted her a pair of silver earrings. Everyone laughed it off, but I brought it up with Mark one day, just out of curiosity. We were at the cinema, and while the trailers played, I turned to him as he devoured a hot dog drenched in mustard.

"Are you trying to have sex with Reina?" I asked.

He nearly choked.

"Do you give gifts to *all* of your investors?" I tried instead.

He shook his head, sipping from his large fountain soda, clearing his throat. He wiped his mouth with his sleeve. He whispered into my ear, "Reina is the kind of woman who lives off the thrill of living in her own fantasy. I wouldn't trust a word she says."

Standing beside Reina was Tobias. Now, Tobias was someone who was impossible to forget. A young lad with a baby face and a prominent Adam's apple. Unfortunately, he was a junkie, though he swore he was in recovery. He claimed to suffer from back spasms due to the long hours he spent driving shipping trucks across the Ambassador Bridge. Well, Tobias said he met Mark in the parking lot of Amy's Rehab Centre. Mark said he volunteered washing the institute's laundry every other month. Their meeting was orchestrated *by God,* is what Mark said.

Now, how did Tobias have money to invest if he spent everything on methamphetamines? I overheard him once telling Leon that one night in an underground parking lot of a luxury apartment building, he saw a duffel bag full of money on the ground beside a man lying on his back, bleeding from the side of his head.

"Call the police," the man gurgled, blood and saliva mixing in his mouth. In a state of shock, Tobias ran straight toward the exit, realizing much too late that in all the excitement he'd grabbed the man's duffel bag. When Tobias was out and in the clear, the dying man's helpless expression flashed in his mind. Before he could spiral into a pit of guilt and shame, a truck passed by with a large red bumper sticker. JESUS LOVES EVEN SHIT LIKE YOU. Tobias called Mark right away.

Tobias's arms were crossed as he sized up the graphs from over Mark's shoulder.

To the left of Mark was Nelly. That *poor* woman. Her son was only eight years old when he died from a severe peanut allergy. One stormy afternoon when Nelly was feeling particularly low, she got off the bus a stop too late. Thankfully, Mark was in the bus shelter with an umbrella.

"Have you heard the word of God?" he asked her, reaching for her hand.

Nelly was on a folding chair, wearing brown corduroys and a khaki sweater, in our semicircle around the computer. She bit her nails, staring at the screens, sighing every few minutes. Beside Nelly, on a bar stool, was Larry, and I was worried about Larry sitting so high. I was very fond of the man. He was a delight, but I wondered if there was a legal guardian or service worker Mark should've spoken to before accepting any of Larry's money.

The last of the Original Batch was a seemingly "normal" fellow called Muthu, who happened to be one of "ours." Born a Protestant, he decided to give the Evangelicals a try after being moved by a lively sermon one day. Muthu had a mustache and a crown of thick black hair round the perimeter of his polished brown head. He wore a burgundy dress shirt and blue jeans. He was saving to sponsor his wife and daughters, asylum seekers waiting in Siberia.

Mark made it clear to each investor how things would work and what to expect. He would take deposits and execute day trades. Within a reasonable time period, no less than three business days, investors would receive a return on investment (ROI) of at least 10 percent. That was his guarantee, and according to the Original Batch, Mark kept his word.

From the doorway, I had a panoramic view of the room. As self-assured as Mark could be, his leg bounced under the desk. He wiggled his fingers, he gripped the mouse tightly, the veins on his hands bulging, running up his sleeve. Beads of sweat rested on his philtrum. He mumbled under his breath. Completely absorbed by the graphs, occasionally jotting down numbers in his notebook. In his pitches to prospective clients, he projected calm and certainty, but watching him trade was more nerve-racking than watching a child learn to walk around sharp edges.

“Something’s happening,” whispered Reina under her breath. The room was quiet but for the sounds of the computer fan, Larry’s heavy breathing, and Tobias’s feet marching over the carpet as he paced behind Mark.

Mark reclined in the office chair with his arms crossed, brow furrowed and low.

“There it is,” he whispered.

“What? What is it?” asked Muthu.

No one was quite sure what to look for or what to say.

How loud to speak, in case the slightest intervention ruined all our hopes and prayers.

Mary put a finger on her lip, glancing over at Muthu.

"Like I said from the gecko, the trend is your friend, and there she is," replied Mark with a grin, still consumed by the screens.

"What do we do now?" inquired Muthu.

"We go for it. Go for it, man!" Tobias raised his voice, shaking Mark's shoulders from behind his chair.

"Listen. You only live once in this one life. Marry rich or get rich trading. Profit over losses, people," said Mark assuredly.

"Praise God," whispered Reina with her hand high.

"Eh—eh—amen," praised Larry.

"You gotta learn how to take a loss, all right? Buy low, sell high, know the market. This stuff can get technical, but if you don't take a swing, you'll never know a hit. Winners win and losers lose. It's a mindset. A way of life, ya hear me? If the money isn't pouring, we're doing something wrong, and that trend right there. That's the one."

Reina nearly had an orgasm in her seat. Leon and Larry had their eyes closed, either asleep or in prayer, and Muthu, bless him, relentlessly tried to understand the graphs on Global Freeze, finally choosing to trust in Mark's genius instead. The hysterics made me crave a cigarette.

"If there's anything you need to remember, it's this, all right? It ain't about how much you lose, it's about how much you can lose and then still buy again. Someone write that down."

Reina transcribed in her notebook.

"Now, everyone, keep quiet," instructed Mark as he made a call on his Ericsson. He held a hand over his Bluetooth earpiece the eight of us unsure of what to expect.

"Oii! Bobby! It's Mark, Mickey Mark—account three thirteen," he announced in a British accent. "Those candlesticks are singing to me, Bobby. Fucking *Beauty and the Beast* today."

He laughed, making the sign of the cross, mouthing, *Lord, forgive me,* for his foul language. Mark pointed at the graphs, calculating with his finger in the air.

". . . All right, Bobby—that's right. Going short. Five hundred shares and I want to sell. Right now. Now! Buy! Buy! Shit. Fuck. Sell. Sell, goddamn it! Sell!"

Mark made the sign of the cross another three times. He sat on the edge of his seat. Both hands on his head, he turned toward his left shoulder.

"Pray," he whispered.

The Original Batch extended their arms toward Mark and the computer. Mary stood and placed a hand on the monitor. The computer fan hummed.

"Bobby? . . . Bobby. Just say it. Give it to me straight. Give me all you got!"

Mark hit the table. His eyes were closed. He massaged his temples. He leaned back in his chair until finally he cracked a smile, before ending the call.

"You'll never meet a guy like me if you live to be two

hundred. To God be all the glory. We got our money, baby!" Mark raised both hands in the air.

The Batch praised the Lord. Mary, Larry, and Tobias spoke in other tongues, and as eyes were held shut in that moment of fellowship, Mark peeked over at me in the doorway. His gimlet eye caught my stare. I knew I ought to keep watching. Keep watching him closely.

John Gotti –

I thought u said u were good at checkers?

Hustle Baby –

You ask a lot of questions

John Gotti –

LOL

U say interesting stuff

Everything all right?

Hustle Baby –

Since my merch got raided

My guys aren't sending my shipment now

The feds started random inspections at my warehouse

John Gotti –

I didn't kno they were on u this hard

Hustle Baby –

Locked out of my spot

Guys already capitalized in my absence

Copying my exact business model too

John Gotti –

Goddamn it!

Ur such a cutie

Hustle Baby –

I'm being serious here

John Gotti –

Oh I kno!

Create a new demand, create ur own market

Find a surplus and sell it. Go big. Go hard.

They don't call u Hustle Baby 4 nothing, do they?

Hustle Baby –

If they got us suckers buying water –

John Gotti –

There ya go!

That a girl

@– – –>

Hustle Baby –

What's that?

John Gotti –

The rose? It's 4 u

Hustle Baby –

Don't be weird

Be real with me

John Gotti –

Lol

Who isn't their realest on the internet, kiddo?

Another round?

MARY

NOVEMBER 6

It was a miracle. I had new friends. And when they came to our house, they brought gifts as sweet as the frankincense and myrrh brought to the manger in Bethlehem. I worried they would notice what we lacked around the house, but they too were lacking and still gave with joy and open hearts. Leon brought meat. Reina her smile. Tobias all sorts of gadgets and furnishings. Nelly made lemon bars with a coconut crust she said were her son's favorite recipe. Muthu made one of the greatest rasams I've ever tasted. Tangy with the perfect dash of coriander. And Larry brought a bag of cherries. Some hazelnuts. Some gooseberries too. Meeting Mark was a blessing to our home and family.

Dilo was frying an egg in the yellow duck slippers Reina had brought her.

"Don't spend the two hundred dollars Mark gave you, okay? Don't spend any money. Whatever you get, just buy what we need. I'll worry about the rest. And if these clowns start making loads of cash through trading, whatever. You start buying stuff, people start thinking we have money we don't actually have. Look at all this stuff Tobias got us. A back massager. Six-slice toaster. Those damn blue headlights. Who the hell needs blue headlights—"

"Adiye, make your egg and eat your egg. I need that two hundred for work supplies."

That child spoke too much for having that many pimples on her forehead. I dipped a cream biscuit in my tea, sitting at the table watching the child I birthed pick her nose looking out the window. Wiping her finger in the sink. *Chi.* Anji for once was at least feeding Maysha at the table. Minced meat and rice. Minced meat and rice she scooped, mashed, and rolled gracefully into bite-sized balls with her fingers. Meat provided by Leon.

"Maysha, want scrambled eggs?" she asked.

"Hell no!" shouted Maysha.

I felt a *verry* strong migraine coming. Believe me. I worried so much about our girls.

"How long will you be rotting at home before you bring something to this table?" I asked Anji, sick and tired of seeing that woman without purpose.

"Do you think Mark would be in our lives if it weren't for me?"

This woman who decided to use her body and charm before using her logic and reason had the nerve to ask me such a question. Really and truly, sometimes too much schooling brought a nasty character out of people. One that sat on a high horse with a kundi stuffed with jasmine, and had an inability to talk to normal people. My God! I managed my temper with the women in my house by the grace of the Lord. I looked right at Anji, and I pointed my finger in her face.

"Mark came to our home because I invited him. These blessings had nothing to do with you. The owner of the biscuit factory has chains and cages for children. Coloring books too. I can book a cage once you start working. Maysha can stay at the factory with me, no? Just get a bloody job, because these children need to eat and Mark is not their father."

Anji rolled another ball of rice and mince with her hand, looking down at the plate. Not even a peep out of her.

I met Dilo near her school and we were on the 134 Nugget bus to the factory shop to pick up my work uniform, boots, gloves, and hairnets. All that I needed to work safely and meet factory standards.

Dilo was seated beside me on the window side. I knew she was thinking. She made a particular face when she wondered too much for her age. That same face she made staring out from her cot when she was a baby. She thought too much, too often.

"Did you really sell your thaali?" she asked.

"You ask too many questions."

"Just don't sell nothing no more, okay?"

"What are you talking?"

"To Mark. For trading. Don't get involved."

"You don't worry about me, pillai. When I have my own

money, God will tell me. But Mark is making money, no? You can make a million dollars in one year day trading, did you know?"

"I gave out résumés—"

"You're fifteen—"

"I'll be sixteen soon. We don't need him," she replied before turning back to the window.

The Lord has said, even if you have faith the size of a mustard seed, you can move mountains. Life is spectacular when you have comfortable steel-toe boots and a quality worker's jacket with double stitching. I praised the Lord for how we were blessed.

Hustle Baby –

Ur looking at the newest hustler in the Gadgets and Household items department

John Gotti –

That a girl!

Hustle Baby –

Made about 200 bucks selling stuff to moms in a parking lot before end of school pickup

Got 40 bucks for a six–slice toaster

90 for a blender

John Gotti –

U found ur target!

New supplier?

Hustle Baby –

Yeah, I guess so

John Gotti –

Got some good news 2

Opening a new branch in a couple weeks

Lots of holiday bookings coming thru

Hustle Baby –

Christmas paintball?

John Gotti –

Red & green paint, just like u said.

Thinking 2 start military training, summer camp fests, would be cool 2 open up 4 field trips but gotta find the right angle for schools

Hustle Baby –

Anger management

John Gotti –

Damn!

That's good

Lol

Hustle Baby –

Send me your first check, Gotti

;)

John Gotti –

Take u out 2 a nice buffet

Take u somewhere swimming

Book you a room at Gotti Tower on the 59th floor

I'd have so much fun with u

DILO

I couldn't tell you how many returns the Original Batch received from Mark by November 12. Honestly, I couldn't keep up with the pace, even if they called me Hustle Baby. I tried my best to understand Mark and his day-trading operation, but I couldn't get past the fact that people trusted the guy. He could barely speak in complete sentences, but people believed in him enough to hand him their money and then hope for more in return. It all seemed a little sketchy to me, him meeting his guarantee *every time*. At least 10 percent of what was invested? But he made the returns happen, and he did so every few days; it was no wonder we called it a miracle.

Where I grew up, the Jamaicans called Mark's species of male humanoid a "waste man." The kinda man who shouldn't have any responsibilities, but unfortunately he does. He ends up screwing over everyone, including himself. Taking up space, taking up time, taking up resources. Waste men had no respect for themselves, so they had no respect for most anything else. Give them nothing, they're a nuisance. Give them power, they become monsters. Give them money *and* power, they become the worst of mankind. If I had an army, we'd be freeing the world of them, one waste man at a time.

I strongly believed that if I tried to understand Mark and the whole trading business that had taken over my room, taken over my life, something would happen to me internally that I would never recover from. So, I let the monkeys be.

I actually learned more during my suspension than I did in school. I learned how to start a fire with zebra shit, how to escape a choke hold, and what to do if there was too much carbon monoxide in your home. But between time spent back in class and the investor sessions, which were daily occurrences in my room, my personal time to surf the web was shrinking fast. Before, I could hop directly from my bed to the office chair in front of the computer, the ideal situation. I'd never enjoyed dallying indoors for longer than three consecutive hours, unless I was sleeping. But now, with the internet within arm's reach, I indulged my curiosity, blissfully led down infinite pathways. The rabbit holes that hyped me more than Toaster Strudels on a Sunday concerned survival. I was preparing for the inevitable collapse of society. I *needed* my time back.

That Sunday after church, even though the market was closed for the weekend, the Original Batch and them were back in my room analyzing Global Freeze. The temperature was five degrees, so I threw a toque on before heading to the backyard for some survival training. I punched the tire a couple times with my bare fists. I read online about the benefits of building calluses. I practiced strikes with the machete, controlling my wrists, keeping each cut tight and within shoulder width. I was working on my aim with our Nail Gun Pro when I heard the back door slide open.

"Dilo, what you up to out here by yourself? Is that a target? Let me have a shot." Tobias walked over, flailing his arms excitedly.

His limbs dangled like a daddy longlegs's in his leather jacket and jeans. He touched the nails on the target board with the back of his hand. Mark followed. He held a cigarette between his fingertips, which he'd lit by the time he realized he was in the line of fire. His eyes were cold and cutting looking into mine. I turned the other way before he did. Reina zipped up her pink puffer jacket, trailing behind. She was probably Anji's age, maybe a little younger, even if she had teenagers for kids. I was never good at guessing people's ages.

"You know how to hold the thing right?" I asked Tobias before passing him the nail gun as his feet straddled the shooting line. He rolled his shoulders back.

"I got one of these at home," he said.

Mark crouched to eye the nail gun in Tobias's hands.

"The tool for the everyday man, that's what they call it, right?"

He took a long, exaggerated draw from his cigarette.

"There's that scene in *Lethal Weapon*—" he continued, blowing smoke from his lips.

"Oh my God, that's my favorite movie!" chimed Reina, buttering up Mark like she did.

Tobias took deep breaths, standing square to the target, squinting like a sharpshooter.

"What's the distance on this? Fifteen meters?" he asked, holding the nail gun out with two hands in front of him.

"Twelve. Just don't hit the fence."

"What kinda loser would hit the fence?" laughed Mark. Reina touched his elbow and laughed with him. Mark inched closer to Tobias, sizing him up as he tried to focus. Tobias, unfazed, was deciding whether to trust his use of the sight or fire instinctively. Shooting was complex. It was no joke. I didn't mind the meticulous approach, but Tobias was taking his sweet-ass time.

"I thought you said you had one of these," I said.

"Never tried anything crazy like this, though."

Tobias was really enjoying himself. I'd never noticed that he had a chip in his tooth. Thick, dark eyebrows, too. If I had to guess I'd say he was in his twenties. Maybe twenty-three. Not much older than me. I didn't notice that he got me smiling. Maybe I blushed. I don't know, but Tobias was a nice guy, and he was into shooting. We shared a laugh. Nothing serious. But then Mark shoved Tobias like some kinda gorilla. Grunting and all.

"All right, just shoot the damn thing!" hollered Mark, with the cigarette hanging between his lips. He grabbed the nail gun from Tobias's grip.

"Oh, come on, man," Tobias complained.

Mark got away with not being a nice person because he performed miraculous acts, but I wouldn't let that slide. Tobias stepped back, crossing his arms behind him, as Mark took up as much space as possible on my shooting line. Trying too hard. He held the nail gun up with one hand. Then the moron positioned it sideways. But nail guns weren't handguns. Nail guns were heavy. Mark was a waste man. A wannabe. A show-off.

Drooping, dropping.

Pew

A nail hit the lower left target.

Drooping, dropping.

Pew

A nail hit the fence. It was almost impressive to miss by that much. The guy was an embarrassment.

"Good job, Mark," said Reina. She smiled as Mark walked away rubbing his shoulder, mumbling to himself.

"The wind, man. The wind messes with the trajectory. You should look into that, kid. Sure isn't safe to shoot on days like today," he said, handing the nail gun back to Tobias. Mark rubbed his hands and blew on his cold fingers. He avoided looking in my direction at all costs until he realized how that made him out to be. A clown. A loser, and Mark just could not lose. He was annoying, all right. He turned straight at me, taking steps closer until he was in my face, and I could smell his breath. Dill pickles and tobacco. A hint of a strawberry sweet.

"You gotta wax your mustache soon, eh?" he said.

He threw his cigarette carelessly toward our purple maple tree. Landed near my tire, an inch beside one of Maysha's plastic toy cars, the color faded from years of precipitation.

"Hey! A single cigarette butt can set a whole house on fire, ya goof," I said.

Mark sneered.

"Well, then be a doll and pick it up, will ya? I gotta make us all some money."

He walked back toward the house.

Once you meet a waste man, you'll start to notice them everywhere.

Pew
Pew
Pew

I fired off three shots. Two nails on the bull's-eye. The other just an inch below. Too windy, my ass.

NOVEMBER 12

We were at the Way of Truth Evangelical Church, again, on a breezy Sunday. Brother Larry was in the crowd at the altar, eager to share his testimony. I'd heard Brother

Larry tell Muthu and Nelly that he wanted to proclaim, from every street corner, just how great God was to him. Mark had made the Original Batch three returns that week and the group was in high spirits. Mark had gotten a lot of investor interest after his last testimonial a couple weeks back, so he was all for Larry telling the church about the miraculous new day-trading business.

Among the many people waiting at the altar was a couple standing behind their son, who was seated in a wheelchair, a look of uncertainty on his face. And then like lightning flashing from the east to the west, lights trained in on the crowd. The entire church fell silent. Larry was the first one chosen to bear witness. It was time for the testimonies.

The pastor had his hand on Larry's shoulder. Larry looked a little nervous. He was a trove of fascinating facts and unbelievable stories, but his condition made public speaking difficult. He'd practiced all week in anticipation of the spotlight and wore his favorite bowling shirt and olive slacks, his hair combed to one side with a pinch of grease.

"Good morning, brother! What a glorious day the Lord has made. Tell us who you are and why you're at the altar this morning. The usher says you have two miracles to share. Is that right?"

"Y-yes, Pastor. La—La—Larry is ma name."

"And how good was the Lord to you this week, Brother Larry? Tell us of your first blessing."

The congregation sat on the edge of their seats.

“Ga-ga-gahd healed me of ma-ma sta-sta-stutter—”

Ceiling lights illuminated the sweat that pearled on Larry’s nose. The pastor’s skin glimmered on the right screen. Powdered and rosy. The drummer rolled softly on the snare. Pastor Todd eyed the usher who’d invited Brother Larry to the front, pulling a white handkerchief from inside his suit pocket, wiping the back of his neck. He gripped Larry’s shoulder tighter and smiled.

“Glory to God for His healing, brother. What else has the Lord done for you?”

“He ba-ba-blessed me financially.”

“Praise to our King. Is that your tithe in your hand there, brother? That envelope you brought with you?”

Larry nodded, handing the envelope to the pastor.

“Ma—ma extra earnings,” he said, raising his voice and standing tall, because Larry had really waited all week for this. He fell on a knee, although it wasn’t clear if it was on purpose. The church gasped. Larry picked himself back up as the pastor held the envelope up before the congregation. He placed a hand on Brother Larry’s head.

“Malachi three, verses eight to ten, church. Recite these words as you work this week. For the Lord said, ‘Bring the whole tithe into the storehouse.’ Test Him and see just how much He will open the floodgates of heaven onto you and pour more blessings than you have any room for!”

Larry’s head leaned back. He took steps backward, the pastor’s hand nearly covering the top of Larry’s face.

“Glorrry to God!” the pastor exclaimed, and Larry

fell in submission to the Lord, on his back at the altar, and the drummer crashed the cymbals as the choir praised. The pastor raised his hand, and the church was silent again but for the drummer, rolling softly on the snare.

The pastor held Larry's envelope to a camera. He poked his thumb through the seal and slid the envelope open. The camera zoomed in on a shot of his chubby fingers, decked in golden rings, digging in the envelope. He pulled out a ten-dollar bill. Bright and purple. Crisp and smooth. The congregation gasped.

"Praise the Lord for our dear brother, church. Praise the Lord for our dear brother, church!"

The church got to their feet. Hands raised. The organ played.

"God Almighty blessed our brother with two glorious miracles this week, and we pray, in Jesus's holy name, that in the days to come our brother Larry will be blessed more abundantly, that he will have no room to contain the mercy of God. Glory hallelujah! Sing, church, sing!"

The orchestra roared on as the lights brightened and the congregation praised their God. Golden plates were passed between pews, and the people sang for manna to fall from the sky.

Hustle Baby –

Ur taking ages to move

You're not even trying to win

Hello?

John Gotti –

Sorry HB

Hustle Baby –

Are u doing something else?

John Gotti –

Am I talking 2 other girls?

Hustle Baby –

Are you working or something?

John Gotti –

Haven't bin feeling 2 well 2work

U kno how it is with Christmas next month

The damn election recounts

Hustle Baby –

Tell me about it

Try 2 take it easy

John Gotti –

What u wearing?

Hustle Baby –

Nothing much, just a tux

John Gotti –

Yeh, yeh

What's under the tux

Hustle Baby –

. . .

John Gotti –

Ever since u told me u had double ds tho . . .

;)

Hustle Baby –

Focus, Gotti

It's your turn

John Gotti –

:D U know I luv talking to u HB

The internet wouldn't b the same without u

ANJI

I never worried about how my disdain for men and state power could influence the girls under my care. I taught them to defend themselves, not to commit violence, *first*—unless the sword was at their necks—that choosing aggression before thoughtful conversation was a sign of weakness. I taught our girls to be tactful and strategic. To manage their emotions in the face of adversity and temptation, and to always consider the greater good. I preached these messages repeatedly because I believed in a ruthless vanguard who in due time must disintegrate hierarchies and hand the reins back to the people. The people who, by then, would be better prepared, trained, and empowered to manage themselves collectively. An end to rampant individualism! An end to war!

I kept a manifesto I'd written in a drawer. The last few lines read:

We're running out of time.

lobotomías o muerte!

lobotomies or death!
Or pave a path toward liberation.

Mark lounged on the new La-Z-Boy Tobias had gifted us. Maysha was on his lap watching *Heat*. The glare from the new thirty-six-inch flat-screen television lit their faces, and if I'd had my camera I might have taken a picture, if I weren't already in such a foul mood.

I'd been pacing since we arrived home from Sunday service, stopping occasionally at the vanity. Who was that woman looking back at me? I walked back to the living room and faced Mark, ready to confront him about what had been troubling me.

"He made us look like fools up there," I started, biting my finger.

"This is a great movie. This is *so* fucking good," said Mark, pointing at the screen.

"Mark. He made us look like fools up there," I repeated.

"Anji. I don't think you understand how great this movie is. It's one of my favorites. Dilo had the DVD all along. Not even an original copy, but look at the quality."

"Mark. Pay attention to what I'm saying. Larry made us look like fools up there."

"You're still banging on about that?"

Mark paused the movie. Maysha cuddled beside him.

"Yes, I'm still 'banging on' about that. What happened is bad for business."

"Bad for business? I'm doing God's work, sweetie. Take it easy and come sit down."

Maysha tugged at Mark's shirt, beginning the first act of her new tantrum routine, which, unfortunately, was very effective. She wailed at an excruciatingly high pitch. She had incredible tenacity. I wondered if she challenged herself, with each successive tantrum, to sustain an even more annoying sound.

"Maysha," I said sternly. "Don't you dare start that again."

I leaned forward with my finger out, giving her my most menacing glare.

"You sit right there and wait until we're done talking. Mark will press play when we're ready."

My finger emphatically pierced my words in the air.

Maysha scowled. Maysha didn't whine. Maysha screamed. Maysha spat at me. I really should've slapped her, but of course that was now frowned upon. Mark raised his hands to his ears and made a funny face. His fingers were pincers and inched closer and closer to my chella kanna. Three years old and she kept her guard up high. Maysha tried not to smile. She held her breath so as not to scream. She knew Mark's routine; the Little Monster was about to pounce. She sat on his lap, facing him. My sweet little girl froze in anticipation, with her flower face and sunken eyes. Mark raised a brow. He tickled her. Maysha laughed. She laughed from her belly till she almost cried. He held her tight as if she were his own. She giggled. Her smile was my heart made bare, exposed to the world. Her pain would forever be mine. Her joy could lift my spirit, and I would die every time she was fulfilled. Through my baby, I was born anew.

Maysha snuggled into Mark's arm, against his chest. On the screen, a distinguished Pacino sat opposite a ravishing De Niro in a booth surrounded by people who may have never held a gun. People who may have never stolen because they had to. People who may have never had to run in fear for their lives.

"Mark."

"I had a crazy week, Anji. I thought I could just sit down and watch a fucking movie."

"Just give me two minutes of your time."

Mark was as still as the picture paused on the screen in front of him.

"Mark?"

"I'm waiting for you to say whatever it is you've been trying to say for the last five minutes."

"Larry made us look like idiots, Mark! How many times do I have to say it?"

"He didn't mention my name. No one knows there's any association between us."

"But they will. I thought you wanted to grow your investors."

"Do you see me doing thrill-seeking trades with a 'born to lose' tattoo on my chest?"

"I beg your pardon?"

"Come on, Anji. Larry's testimony won't change a thing. Now, if you're finished, I'd like to continue watching one of the greatest movies of all time—"

"What was I thinking with you?"

"Here we go—"

"You have no idea what you're doing, do you?"

Mark laughed.

"Your mom says all kinds of funny stuff, doesn't she, May?"

Maysha laughed along with Mark. I marched to the television screen and grabbed the DVD cover. A terrible print job of two men I'd gladly lie between in any amount of heat. Faded lines of color across their faces. I put the DVD cover in front of the sensor.

"Oh, come on!"

"Yeah!" shouted Maysha.

"I don't understand why Larry's tithe was only ten dollars. He said that was his whole return."

"What are you asking me, Anji?"

"Did Larry only give you a hundred dollars? Don't lie to me, Mark."

"Calm down, Anji. Larry is clearly not right in the head."

"Mark—"

"I'm sorry, I'm not educated enough to know what his problems are called—"

"So, why did you take his money?"

"I'm trying to tell you, but you keep interrupting—"

"Why do you keep so much hidden from me?"

"Let me finish a goddamn sentence, all right? The Lord spoke to Brother Larry. I had nothing to do with it."

"His ROI was ten dollars and we're calling that a miracle?"

"He made about a thousand dollars."

"Don't lie to me, Mark."

"Sorry, he gave me a thousand dollars. I'm tired. It's late."

"Mark—"

"All right! He gave me eight fifty—"

"I need you to be honest with me, if this is going to work."

"What are you talking about, Anji? I thought I made myself clear. I'm not interested in making anything work if it doesn't pay me, and to be honest, none of this is any of your business . . . Larry is Larry, and either Larry doesn't know how much ten percent is, or he can't count. Maybe he left the rest of his tithe on his nightstand. No one will ever know but God. Not even Larry. So, just sit your ass down and watch the rest of the movie with us, all right?"

Mark made the sign of the cross and held Maysha tighter. She pointed at the screen.

"Your mommy's not done talking, Maysha," he whispered loud enough that I could hear, sweet enough that she laughed.

"You're targeting all the wrong people, Mark."

"Targeting? God speaks to my investors and they come to me. They signed a waiver. Everyone's aware of the risks involved."

"There are people who actually have money."

"One day you'll understand when the Holy Ghost speaks, and when you do—"

"I have an idea," I interrupted.

All some men needed was a little mothering, some guidance, and a pat on the back.

"Listen, Anji. I'm not some random jerk-off. I know what I'm doing, all right?"

"We could be making money, Mark."

"Correction. I *am* making money."

"Well, you could be making more."

I removed the cover from the sensor.

"Watch the movie with us. I'll pray about what you said, and we can talk about it later. You gotta respect a man's time off, all right?"

Mark held the remote up to the television with his thumb hovering over play.

"Can I ask you a question?" I blurted, stood in front of him again. He sighed. "What do you believe in?" I asked.

Mark smiled, leaning his head back on the chair.

"I believe in my Lord."

Mark handed Maysha the remote and pointed out the play button. With a wide grin, my daughter pressed play.

"It's time for bed, *May,*" I said, grabbing her from Mark's arms as she cried and squealed, hitting my back and shoulders, begging to go back in the living room to watch the rest of the film.

John Gotti –

I think today is the day – – –

Hustle Baby –

You're gunna see ur friend Ben?

John Gotti –

– – – u tell me what u look like!

or send me a pic . . .

Something steamy?

Plzzz:(

Hustle Baby –

You never win when first kill is switched off

John Gotti –

Come on!

Tell me! :(

Hustle Baby –

I look like a worm

Like a person

Like a girl

I don't know

Ask me something else Gotti!

John Gotti –

U said u live alone, right?

Hustle Baby –

Yup!

Who do u live with?

John Gotti –

My grandma & her capuchin

Hustle Baby –

You have a capuchin?

Do you have a permit?

John Gotti –

Yes ma'am. Documents and vaccines

I just sent u a picture of him

He's pretending he's drinking tea on my grandma's couch

Pretty cool eh :P

Hustle Baby –

Lol

So cool

John Gotti –

I bet u got a nice laugh

I bet ur really pretty

DILO

What did I think about the new church we were wasting time in? I mean, to each their own. So long as no one was getting killed or taken advantage of, how could a cult bother me? I was just a kid, but I already knew that church wasn't for me.

How can I explain what I felt in places of worship without sounding like a prick? People were nice, I guess. Sickly sweet, hardly a problem. Just trying to be happy. Church was a party most weekends; you were always guaranteed to see people excited to greet you. Good people. Was there anywhere safer than a place where people gathered and surrendered to a power they could not see, and through faith were made vulnerable to belief?

We can't just crawl back into our mothers' wombs and hide, now, can we? Mary asked me that when I was four.

NOVEMBER 26

After Sunday service, Anji was talking to Sister Sheila, who seemed genuinely interested in Anji's Value Village finds. The leather, the fur. The Gucci and Hilfiger she made Mark buy for us at the location in Richman Hill. All of us rocking new secondhand finds. We called it our heavenly armor.

Sheila's husband, Bruce, had the most questions for Anji. Probably about the money she flashed at the altar. She would have been quite the actress, if given the opportunity. Even I believed that she had earned a thousand bucks trading stocks for two straight weeks. And the *heart* she had. Deciding both weeks to give all her earnings to the Lord. What a remarkable woman my aunty was. We were good when we needed to be. Always ten steps ahead of the game.

Four other couples gathered around Anji. Front-pew people. We would call them the Five. The way they dressed—the quality of the fabric, the soft and subtle bling—for sure they had cash they could afford to lose. Mary was standing among the group, too. Hardly looking like an odd one out with what she was wearing. I hadn't seen her smile like that for a while, watching as the couples stood listening to Anji's tales of miraculous earnings. And then there was Maysha. Entertaining all who gave her any attention. Looking as cute as ever in that tulle dress she wore. Her new shy-girl routine won her sweets and head rubs.

Outside, Larry, Tobias, Mark, and I were gathered, as the other members of the Original Batch were in line for refreshments.

"You heard the pastor about that rapture stuff? I'm not messing around anymore," said Tobias with his hands behind his head. His flannel shirt lifted. He had a trail of hair under his belly button that went down into his jeans. A tattoo on the side of his stomach read BORN TO FLY.

"Oh yeah! Jesus is coming and I can feel it," said Mark, looking over at Anji with Sister Sheila and her group of friends, hitting a palm over his fist impatiently.

Anji raised her hand and waved Mark over. She smiled pleasantly, like she and Mark were happily in love and about to get married.

Mark adjusted his tie.

"If you'll excuse me. The Lord is about to bless."

He straightened his secondhand Armani blazer. Grinning like a Ken doll, he retrieved his business cards from his suit pocket. The man was ready.

John Gotti –

You never said.

Do u have a bf?

Hustle Baby –

You never asked

John Gotti –

Do u?

Hustle Baby –

No boyfriend

Wanna play Checkers tag team?

John Gotti –

U ever been kissed?

I bet u got nice lips

Hustle Baby –

I had loadsss of boyfriends

Not worth a kiss

Worried about the rapture tho

John Gotti –

LOL

U don't want 2 b left behind?

Hustle Baby –

If the rapture is real, what if Jesus comes back before u get to do something u've never done but really want to do?

John Gotti –

That's what ur worried about?

Jesus cock blocking u from ur first kiss?

Hustle Baby –

I never said that

John Gotti –

U kinda did

U walking around with lip balm in case the trumpet sounds LOL

That's actually real cute, HB

MARY

I had prayed and visualized exactly what we needed. I saw the money in my hands. I felt every bill. One thousand. Two thousand. Three thousand. Four thousand. Five. The spirit of the Lord reminded me.

> *Therefore, I tell you, whatever you ask for in prayer, believe that you have received it, and it will be yours—*
>
> MARK 11:24

The Original Batch were with Mark visiting open houses on Sixteenth Avenue. New developments where who knows what once grew. A high school had been constructed. An elementary school too. Parks with fountains and soft tracks, and more than one spiral slide. Mark was sure we were in for a great return *verry* soon. I had gone to see one of those open showings with him some days before. Four, five bedrooms, a basement with two, three rooms. I envisioned our entire lives within those walls. The birthday parties. The Christmas dinners. The farewells. The tears. The cars in the driveway. Our treasures filling every corner. In the garage. In the backyard. In a shed. Spilling over into an extra bedroom we would one day build. Every inch of our home.

The ride back in Mark's new BMW wasn't so easy. All the memories I'd made, left in that open house. My perfect life. But as much as I could dream, there was reality slapping my face.

There is a child taking a shit on the carpet.
Your husband left you for a woman with nicer breasts.
You don't speak the same language as the child you birthed.
You don't even remember what a penis looks like—Lord forgive me.
You don't see money until you make it.
There was no money, until there was.

. . . Of course, my faith wavered from time to time. I was also human, no?

I was at the kitchen table with Sheila. Sister Sheila. My friend, Sister Sheila. She had a penthouse suite her father bought her in 1991, an early graduation gift as she studied to be a dental nurse.

Sheila and her husband, Brother Bruce, had two beautiful children. They had a five-year-old boy named Kyle, and a thirteen-month-old girl, Esther, who was on Sister Sheila's lap. The boy was in the backyard with Maysha. Sister Sheila had brought a brown envelope that she kept beside her at the kitchen table. She came as a surprise that Sunday, after service. A knock on the front door at about 3 p.m.

I made tea and set out a plate of strawberry-jam-filled biscuits, and a platter of jackfruit and grapes. Sister Sheila kept her jacket on because she said she was cold. Winter must have been on its way.

"If you called, I would've made you nice foods. I gave you my number, but that's okay."

"Oh yes. That's right. Mark said his house was under renovation," she said, clicking the buttons on her BlackBerry pager. A newer version than Mark's.

"Yes, yes. This is my home. You like the tea?"

"Oh, I don't take sugar, I thought I said. So, Mark doesn't live here?"

"No, not sugar. That is condensed milk."

Sister Sheila put her BlackBerry on the table.

"Does Mark stay here with you?" she asked again.

"One day. Only God knows. You need grapes. Look at your skin. Beautiful but you need sugar, no?"

"I have honey in my tea in the mornings, and that's all the sugar for me," she said, and she laughed.

"You are *soo* bad," I said, laughing with her.

"Are you sure you can see the kids back there?" she asked, squinting toward the sliding door.

"Yes, yes. I seeing."

My God. My heart. With some people, really, my English, it crumbles. Sister Sheila must've thought, *Who is this stupid woman?* Ha. Really. I managed, though.

I stood from my chair to draw the curtains back some more. I opened the window so we could hear. I slid the back door open. Maysha was by the purple maple tree watching Sister Sheila's boy, Kyle, push the hanging tire back and forth.

"This won't take long anyway. I was just so amazed by your sister's testimony. Her entire story. A *deep* sinner too," whispered Sister Sheila.

"Praise the Lord. She is a sinner no more, she is saved."

"Praise God! She wore a beautiful dress last Sunday."

"We have very nice selections."

"A Calvin Klein. And the purse?"

"Also, *verry* nice."

"Louis Vuitton. And Mark had that Armani jacket. I haven't seen one on the market in fifteen years."

"We are blessed, praise God."

"Praise the Lord."

Sister Sheila raised a hand for Jesus.

"Well, I spoke to my husband. I prayed ever since that first week when Sister Angel was saved. I thought maybe she taught yoga with her figure. My studio is always looking for new teachers, by the way. And then her testimony touched my heart. And the way the spirit moved inside her. I pride myself on being a good judge of character. My parents are both psychologists."

"Yes. Yes. Praise God. Do you like the jackfruit? This is from my country. Please, please, try."

That woman didn't touch her tea. She didn't touch the biscuits. She didn't touch a single fruit.

"I really am so proud of our church. All of Pastor's work. Bringing in someone like Mark. Changing his trajectory. Finding people like you."

"Yes. Yes. Praise God. How about a grape? Please. One grape, Sister Sheila."

"We're really hoping to open new churches around the world. Spread the message of truth. They're building a church in Cancún, did you know? We'll have our own little spot."

And just as we were becoming great friends, I noticed an eyelash on the side of my fruit platter. I nearly fell backward on my chair.

Pew
Pew

Sister Sheila shot up, holding her drooling baby. She ran out the sliding back door. Having heard the Tamil Radio blasting bullets and shelling every day, I hardly heard the gun. I hardly heard the birds. Ha! I'm laughing. Maysha and Kyle were in the backyard, as I knew. But, praise the Lord, Dilo was with them.

"Is that a gun?" asked Sheila from the patio.

"It's a Nail Gun Pro," shouted Dilo.

"Only a nail gun. Not a *real* gun," I reassured Sister Sheila.

"Look at all the nails, Mommy," said Kyle, pointing at

the target. Happy to be in our home. Kyle touched maybe twenty nails. Maybe thirty. Stroking the metal heads as if they were made of fur.

Sister Sheila was a busy woman. It was nice they stopped by. She was in such a hurry. Grabbing the children. Grabbing her bag. Rushing with their shoes. Thankfully, I managed, as quickly as possible, to pack the jackfruit for her children. They could eat at home, no? I gave a container to Sheila, and she handed it to her boy. I thought, wow, this boy was so trustworthy. Even at five. Maysha would've thrown the dish and run off while shitting in her pants. Knowing our girl, laughing all the while.

"Please tell Mark we had a great time. And, please, please, give him that envelope," she said, smiling.

As they walked to their car, only a few steps away, Sister Sheila's boy dropped the container of jackfruit on the ground. Soft yellow seashells tumbled onto our greasy driveway one at a time.

"Don't worry. You go. I will clean. Don't worry. You go, sister. You go with peace."

My Lord. I thought the skin on my face would peel and drop on our porch. That jackfruit came from Malaysia through Anji's friend Yusuf, who sold fruit from the back of his van.

"Oh, thank you. God bless you," she said, waving.

At least she didn't notice the hair on my platter, because if she had, she'd have run off with the envelope too. Ha. I'm only joking.

As soon as Sister Sheila's car was out of sight, well down

and out of our street, as soon as Maysha was comfortable in front of the TV again, I went to the kitchen and put the kettle on. As the water boiled, I opened the envelope. I almost fainted. If Mark asked who had opened the seal, I would blame it on Maysha. She was out of hand and nearly tore the whole house down. He wouldn't be the wiser.

Five couples. Five bundles too. Ten one-hundred-dollar bills kept with paper clips. Five kutti stacks under my roof, on our table. Five thousand dollars in cash was in our house—just like that. Just as I'd prayed. God was revealing Himself to me. Our money was coming. In Jesus's mighty name.

John Gotti –

Not sure how long I'll be at my spot

Hustle Baby –

You're moving out?

John Gotti –

New location looks promising

May be worth it 4 me 2 move closer

Hustle Baby –

What about ur monkey?

John Gotti –

U want 2 meet my monkey? ;)

Hustle Baby –

Hell yeah!

John Gotti –

LOL

Wish u were here right now

Pop out sum brewskies

Sit on my lap

Watch movies all night long

My hands all over u

mmm

. . . ain't no box like urs HB

DILO

DECEMBER 5

In our house, you ate when food was available or you'd be sorry, especially if the food was *really* good. You got your ass up when you were summoned for something to eat.

We needed five thousand dollars, and I was starting to think the rest of the house had forgotten. I had no idea where I'd get the money, but I just wanted to keep my room, and my stuff. Spend a few more years in our backyard.

I asked around to see what I could hustle up. I knew some guys at school, who knew some *serious guys,* who needed *serious things,* more than what I had at my disposal. There was a world of people on the internet, but I mainly dealt with kids from schools in Scarborough. I found a guy who wanted a flat-screen; ours wasn't plasma, but it was a thirty-six-inch, and that would have to do. The other guy was looking for a DVD player. Luckily, I had that too. I'd have to move it quick; maybe I'd make it look like we got robbed or something. We were nearing the end of the semester, and I still had a long list of assignments to worry about on top of finding five grand.

Mark was at the kitchen table making goofy faces at Maysha. Each with their own bowl of pomegranate in front of them. My bowl was across the table from Mark. So, that's where I sat. Larry and Nelly stood by the sliding back door looking out the window with their own bowls too. Each of ours evenly portioned. We counted seeds.

Ding

In my mad dash to get the last bowl of pomegranate, I'd left my window open on the computer by mistake. I must've yanked my headphones from the speaker when I hopped from my chair. My chat notifications were loud, but hopefully no one would notice I was in the middle of organizing a sale.

Ding
Ding

The acid in my stomach gurgled. Anji was out back with Muthu and Leon. All three experienced shooters. I hadn't realized the Batch was already at our house.

Mark's briefcase was on the floor against the wall behind him. Maysha stood on her chair with a spoonful of pomegranate in her mouth. She climbed across the table and crawled closer to me, her sticky hands all over the articles I'd printed out. She cocked her head and poked her finger in my eye. She laughed when I shouted at her. She screamed when I smacked her arm. She crawled to Mark and sat on his lap. He bounced her up and down. He blew a raspberry on her shoulder. He said, "Now, you be a good girl. A sweet girl, and we'll all get ice cream later."

"I'd love some ice cream," said Nelly.

"Me too," added Larry.

"Then that's what we'll do," said Mark, hitting the table with two hands. Our spoons rattled.

I knew he was looking over at me. Waiting for a reaction. I hated when adults did that. Needing acknowledgment for doing the bare minimum, things any decent human being should do. That desperation.

"What's that in front of you?" asked Mark, spooning some pomegranate into his mouth.

"What? In front of who?"

"Those papers you brought with you. On the table. What you're reading now."

Ding
Ding

Each chime tugging at my mind, pulling me back to my desktop. Someone needed me. Someone cared what I thought. I was a somebody, in their mind. I needed to get back to the computer, before I missed something important. Possible clients, I mean.

Mark and Maysha stared from across the table. Maysha threw a pomegranate seed in my direction.

"I just printed some stuff—" I said to Mark.

He stretched across the table for a better look.

"'Capuchin Husbandry'? 'How to Escape a Kidnapping'? 'How to Survive Internal Bleeding'? You need someone to talk to, kid?"

His voice was serious. Concerned. None of this was his business. And then a laugh fell out of his mouth like the laugh was a rat that climbed out from his stomach. He thought I was funny?

"'Capuchin Husbandry'? 'How to Escape a Kidnapping'?" he repeated faintly.

Two excellent articles I'd found, read, saved, and printed, to annotate later.

I shifted my body away, shielding my papers from sight. We weren't allowed to eat in our rooms, otherwise I'd have left to eat in peace. I didn't mind Mark some days. We talked about movies and music. How to make a million dollars and what we'd do with that money. I wouldn't say he felt like an uncle; he was less than a brother, not quite a friend. Just a guy who was at our house, too often, spending time with the women in my family. A guy who, I must admit, actually helped make things a little better. However, when he had nothing to distract him, he chose to annoy me. His laptop had overheated and was charging, so I guess he had nothing better to do.

"What got you interested in capuchins?" he asked.

Ding
Ding

"Were you the last one on the computer?" asked Mark.

Ding

"Dilo, I'm talking to you . . . Don't give me that cut-eye, kid . . . Don't kiss your teeth at me either," he said under his breath, hawk eyes on me.

Mary walked into the kitchen from the shower.

"It's rude to ignore your friends, Dilo," said Mark, helping himself to another spoonful of glass-red seeds, from Maysha's bowl this time.

Ding

"She doesn't even read her Bible, Mark. How many times have I asked that child to memorize Psalm 91? What do you expect?" said Mary, drying her hair with a towel.

Ding

Anji walked in from the backyard, smelling of tobacco.

"What's going on?" she asked, passing between Larry and Nelly to wash her hands.

Ding
Ding

"Whose messenger is that?" she asked, scrubbing her hands with soap.

"My friends from school. We have a project," I said, standing from my seat.

"Sit down," ordered Anji.

I stood right where I was.

"Are you in a public chat room?" she asked, shaking her hands out to dry.

"No—"

"Look me in the eyes and tell me the truth, or I'll go in your room and find out for myself."

"It's Kili from school! We have a project on Costa Rica, for fucksakes. What do you think I'm reading about capuchins for? Just leave me alone!" I shouted in her face.

Mark stood up right away.

"I've checked her account. She's telling the truth. I helped print some of that stuff out for her project," he said.

His hands on Anji's forearm, he gave her a gentle stare. I realized I'd never seen them touch. He put his hand on her cheek and smiled. He asked her for some tea. He turned round when Anji put the kettle on. Looking at me. Waiting for a reaction. I went to my room and slammed my bedroom door shut. Hopefully, they'd leave me alone.

John Gotti –

All right now ur taking ages to move

Come on HB

Where R u?

Hustle Baby –

I hate people

I hate people so much

John Gotti –

Whoa

What happened?

U hate everyone?

Hustle Baby –

People suck

John Gotti –

They suck balls

But some people r all right

Don't u think?

Hustle Baby –

:(

John Gotti –

Keep ur cool, cutie

Don't let them get you down

Ur 2 sweet to b sad

Let's finish this game

I gotta get back 2 work soon

Hustle Baby –

I'm gunna meet ur monkey
right?

John Gotti –

U have my word, baby

ANJI

The thought of a man in my life ignited a terrible feeling. I hardly slept. I hardly ate. My conundrum wasn't whether Mark loved me or not. Rather, I worried about time. The passing time. The time passing. The time I could be using to do something else. I could almost hear the ticking of each second.

I was capable of taking care of myself, but suppose my life was in jeopardy and my survival was somehow dependent on the choices a man had to make on my behalf? The terror. And then I had my usual worries: When would I discover I had a terrible disease? When would I no longer be able to orgasm, and would I even miss that euphoric titillation? When and how would my world crumble into pieces? And how long after that storm would I begin to feel "fine" again?

A starlit sky. The night is still. Saguaro cacti watch from eight feet high. I am in a desert pond, and the smell of white brush envelops me as Sonoran Desert toads croak a stellar symphony. He swims to me. The water parts. A touch. A spark. He grabs me in his arms. Ripples in the water. I wrap my legs around his torso. I hold him around his neck, pushing myself closer and closer to his heart. I drip for him. His heart thumps against my chest. Slippery skin. I feel myself soften for his everything. Moaning in his ear. Salty droplets in my mouth. I suck his lobe. My lips along his neck. I nibble. I lick. I kiss. My fingers in his mouth. The otherworldly squish of his tongue.

He moans for me.

I can leave this dream. I have gotten all I need.

My hormonal fluctuations led me down foolish pathways teetering between "love" and desire and pain. Still, I knew what Mark had to offer. I knew what to expect from the man, which was very little. He was a moron of his own class. A prime candidate for president of the Chimp Society. Love was not in our cards. I assumed he was into uncomplicated "babes." Pretty, simple faces. Entitled and lacking personality. Lacking life experience.

What I suppose I'm trying to say is, I found every second with Mark infuriating. The man had me on edge. He was an absolute embarrassment. And then there was my gut. Suddenly I was irregular. My period arrived ten days too soon. Mentally I felt parts of me slipping, causing friction, sparking my nerves, igniting a readjusting that caused me great confusion. You don't know until you do. When the knife pierces and you bleed.

After November 26, Mark paid for my time in weekly groceries. I was given a weekly stipend of four hundred dollars. He covered our other expenses, too. The fancy secondhand finds. Driving us to and from locations. Quid pro quo, he called me "sweetheart" after my first thousand-dollar testimony. On a few occasions he experimented with "baby." Mark had more investors thanks to me, but he never acknowledged that fact. He thanked the Lord instead.

It was Sunday, December 10. By then, I'd say, the Five had received a few rounds of healthy returns from Mark, the latest earning them each $1,500 from only a five-grand investment. An outstanding 30 percent ROI, by far the largest one yet. That round made Mark feel unstoppable. Even the way he walked changed. The way he spoke and shook hands.

Soon after, Sister Sheila invited Mark and me for dinner along with the rest of the Five. It appeared to be a celebration of our entwined success, but Mark told Sheila that he had a new investment opportunity that he hoped to pitch them. His new real estate endeavor with the half-a-million-dollar houses on Sixteenth Avenue. The open houses he had already invited the Original Batch to inspect. Mark's Realtor friend Sebastian offered an unbelievable deal, but for just another few days. Thirty percent off the listing price, if they would commit today. Mark was enthused to share this opportunity—who wouldn't want to spread the good news—but it was too costly for the Original Batch. None of them had that kind of money lying around. They were normal people.

Sheila's dining room looked like it belonged on the cover of *Chatelaine*. "Women Who Have It All." On an absurdly long table, a variety of dishes and bowls were set. She even had an ornate gold-plated candelabra in the center of the table adorned with crystal-like jewels that hung from each bend. Neatly spaced across the length of her canvas, among the food she had said she "just whipped up on short notice," were antique vases flaunting exotic fern arrangements. Three bottles of wine had been passed around before the first course. Deep red with notes of plum and tangerine, gifts from Sheila's sister's winery in South Africa. On the shelf on the accent wall were handcrafted trinkets from the Maldives. In the china hutch was black, red, and gold lacquerware, and authentic hand-painted porcelain dinner sets. A silver cross with Jesus bleeding from His head was tacked to the wall.

As the other couples filed in along with their expensive aromas, I slipped away to the kitchen, perusing every wall, portrait, and artifact, calculating the cost of being Sheila. I couldn't have been gone for longer than a few minutes, but when I returned everyone was already seated. Two of the men had their napkins on their laps. The women, lipstick on their glasses. At least one person in each couple was surely on medication. Prozac or Zoloft. Perhaps even Lithium. None of which was my business, but between each pair was a red envelope. And from their eager expressions those red envelopes seemed the source of their elation, or had Sheila spiked her filtered water with Valium? Sister Sheila shared a few words.

"Welcome, thank you all for joining me tonight in fellowship. Praise the Lord. I invited you into our home so that we could break bread in honor of our collective success and celebrate the man who was able to lead us to magnificent bounty, Mark."

The Five raised their glasses in unison.

As everyone redirected their attention to Mark, I noticed a not-so-subtle shift in his demeanor. Fidgeting with the table setting. His shoe tapping against the table leg. His behavior similar to how he conducted himself while trading. Normally, in front of the investors, particularly with the Five, Mark exuded an obnoxious cockiness that could make even one of Jesus's disciples want to slap him, but that evening he was unnerved.

"Mark. It's no accident you're here with us. Before you pitch us on your latest investment proposal, we would like to let you know that we are with you. The Spirit has revealed that Christ is working through you. With God by our side, we are more than happy to provide. A proverbial blank check, if you will, a testament to our faith in you and the Lord."

Mark stood up abruptly and excused himself, pointing to his pager, which was clipped onto his belt. His hand cupping his Bluetooth, fastened snug around his ear.

"We'll wait for you," Sister Sheila called after Mark as he marched out of the dining room.

"Always working so hard." She chuckled, taking a sip

from her glass, painfully stretching her cheeks into a smile with fresh units of Botox in her face. Her lips moistened with wine.

Sister Sheila's guest bathroom was equipped with a black Japanese toilet, opposite a shelf with two Bibles and a *Teen Study Bible Guide.* A Tender Moments placard beside a miniature bonsai. *Blessed are the obedient.* A vintage mirror was up against the bold black accent wall behind the sink.

Mark stood on the toilet with his head out the window, smoking a cigarette. Three of his top shirt buttons were undone. Patches of sweat had soaked through the fabric. He exhaled as he leaned out the window. I shut the door gently behind me.

"What the hell is going on, Mark? They're about to start the first course, Bruce said he was hungry."

"I thought I locked the door."

"Well, praise the Lord you didn't."

"Don't do that, Anji. You gotta stop doing that, all right?"

Mark inhaled his cigarette deeply.

"What are you talking about?"

"Using God's name in vain, what do you think?" he snapped.

He blew out smoke from the side of his mouth. He tucked his lips tight, heavily breathing out from his nose, before inhaling again.

"If there was a God, do you think he'd care about such semantics instead of actual issues? 'Oh, Anjali used God's name inappropriately for the fiftieth time this week, we can't let her into heaven now to play the bloody tambourine.' Be serious, Mark. You're losing it."

"You have your beliefs, Anji, and I have mine."

"What has you all worked up, then? You're sweating like a pig."

"You heard what Sister Sheila said."

"All I heard was her singing your praises."

"A proverbial blank check?"

"Do you even know what 'proverbial' means?"

"Do *you,* Anji?"

"Jesus Christ. Listen, Mark, I highly doubt that any functioning adult would give anyone a blank check, let's make that clear."

Mark rolled his eyes.

"But it's all very exciting. After a fifteen-hundred-dollar return in two days, of course the Five want to invest even more with you."

I rubbed his side as he blew more smoke out of the window.

"I was only planning on asking them for another round of five grand. Fuck! Is this the New Jerusalem? Did we make it past the raptor already?"

"Just a minute, Mark. How much do you think is in those envelopes?"

"Ten grand a pop is what Sheila told me. You think I'm in here to pick my ass?"

Mark's leg shook uncontrollably atop the toilet seat, what was left of his cigarette trembling in his hand. Smoke filled the bathroom. Drops of sweat from Mark's forehead fell to the floor. He turned back to face the window, ash softly dusting Sheila's immaculate tiles.

How long had we been gone? I was running out of time. We wouldn't get a better chance than this, and I could feel that as strongly as I felt smoke against my skin. Ten grand per couple guaranteed, and a yahoo woman ready to write up a hefty check if the spirit of God led her. Mark was losing control when it mattered most. Think fast, Anji. Think. Think. How much could I grab before the ship sunk into the sea? We needed five thousand dollars in five days, plus all the debt owed to Mark from incidental expenses. Plus, the sums we planned to send Back Home. The homes for orphaned children. The women's center I hoped to charter. Funding to rethatch roofs and build schools and supply hospital beds for the rural population. Gifts to send back to family who assumed living in a house in Canada came with a sauna and swimming pool, a luxurious life. Point is, we needed that money, and I wouldn't let this gutless imbecile get in my way. Mark was a pig on a spit over hellfire.

"You've kept your guarantee, Mark. You haven't lost anyone a dollar. You've been incredible, wouldn't you say? Maybe this is a test of your faith?"

"Fuck, Anji! Stop with the God shit!"

"But you can do this, is what I'm saying. You have to."

"I don't have that much in circulation! I need a second to fucking think, all right!"

"What do you mean you don't have that much in circulation?"

"What, Anji? What are you talking about?"

"What you just said—"

"I didn't say anything, just now."

"You literally said—you don't have that much in circulation. What the bloody hell does that mean?"

"I never said that. You're twisting my words again."

"What do you mean you don't have that much in circulation? Answer the question, Mark."

"You must have misunderstood me. What I probably meant was that I've never had that much money in one account, all right? I've never traded that much money before. What don't you understand? What I do is harder than you could ever imagine."

Mark stepped down from the toilet and washed his hands with cold water, splashing some on his sweaty skin. He looked up at the mirror, and the fear in his eyes—the situation was that much more delicate.

"I have an idea," I said, turning my back to the window, facing him.

"Of course you do. Trained terrorist over here."

"Excuse me?"

"Give me a break, I have a lot on my mind."

"Make them fishers of men, Mark."

"Why are you so cryptic? Why can't you ever be straight?"

"Pay attention, Mark. Didn't you say you could've taken a course to learn how to trade?"

"Yeah, cost an arm and a dildo."

"But you said it was five grand."

"What's your point, Anji?"

"Offer to teach them a course. Tell them if they bring in more recruits, you'll teach them how to trade for five grand."

"They want to give me ten grand, you nut case."

"Trade the other half. You traded that much from each of them two days ago. You said that's all you wanted."

Mark picked a comb from his back pocket and pulled it through his hair.

"You just came up with that on the spot?" he asked, eyes on his reflection.

"Anyone could have done so, wasn't that tricky—"

He shot a sharp glance at me in the mirror before turning his attention to his eyebrows, tidying their shape.

"What would you do if I just ran off with all the money?" he asked, cracking his knuckles, still facing the mirror, almost posing the question to himself.

"You'd have left me in a sticky situation, that's for sure. All those people. Our friends."

Mark adjusted his collar. He buttoned his shirt up to the top.

"You wouldn't look for me?"

"I don't think you would be that hard to find."

He half smiled. That boyish grin. Terrible when he was two. A menace to his mother. The first woman to let his selfishness slide. The last one to give up on him. I had asked him once about his mother, and he had said he was in no mood to cry.

"I'd be off the coast of Djibouti on a boat playing backgammon with pirates before you even knew I was gone, sweetie," he responded.

"I'm more surprised you've heard of Djibouti. Honestly, I'm impressed."

He was quiet. Still staring at the mirror. Unconcerned by my reflection beside him.

"If you were pulling a scam . . . you'd tell me, wouldn't you, Mark?"

"What?" He laughed.

"You could tell me right now. We could plan this, so no one gets hurt. You leave with more than you had before you entered into our lives. Give me what I'm due and we'll make sure that the Original Batch are secure. Sheila and the Five will survive, but Jesus Christ, Mark. If you are thinking about running, please tell me, Mark!"

He turned his head and walked over to me, looking me in the eyes the entire time. He held my face with both of his clammy hands.

"The fact your brain even went there," he started. "I don't think I've ever met anyone like you, Anji. How could I lie to my partner in crime?"

He kissed my forehead, his hands still cradling my face.

He checked himself in the mirror one last time before heading back into the dining room. Mark was a man with a plan. God's plan. And he was ready to share it with the Five, but I could hear the seconds ticking away.

Tick
Tick
Tick

I was running out of time.

John Gotti –

I think it's time baby!

Hustle Baby –

We already tried Checkers tag team

You wanna play chess?

John Gotti –

No silly!

Be my girlfriend, HB

Hustle Baby –

There are so many girls on the internet

John Gotti –

You're my number 1 tho

Plus . . .

I didn't tell you about my new location

Hustle Baby –

What about it?

John Gotti –

Take u 2 the CN tower?

Go out to see those Jays?

Catch Vince Carter's slam dunks?

Hustle Baby –

I told you what city I live in?

John Gotti –

No

But u said u were an 8-hour drive away

That u watched the Leafs a couple days ago

That the CN tower is overrated

Hustle Baby –

That's pretty smart of you, still

John Gotti –

Lol

Thanks

I'd really like to meet you some day

Ur more than cool HB

MARY

In the months leading up to October 1987, Anji was a rare sighting. This was just before she left for the cold. She was active in schools, helping with the busing, the moving, and the organizing of people. She helped feed women and girls who had come from the Vanni, from the refugee camps. She learned to nurse wounds and sew skin. Naturally, we were terrified about where she may have found herself. *Chi!* So long as that woman lived, her family would worry about her. Every single day. Some women had that tendency.

I knew the smell of blood seeping into mud on a rainy day. Some nights I prayed for another flood. Aiyo kadavuley! Fill our lungs with water if it meant not another child would suffer because of sin and greed. My Lord, all that our children have seen. I prayed the Lord gave them amnesia.

On Sunday night, December 10, Mark and Anji returned from their dinner at Sister Sheila's house. Mark popped open a bottle of Moët in the backyard. He was playful that night. His hands on Anji's arms, on her waist. He hoisted her up. Hugging. They were *touching*! I saw all of this with my own eyes. How he threw her over his shoulder and spun her around under the stars. The moon was full and visible. I watched them from the kitchen window. I was happy, no? I thought maybe they were falling in love.

Mark returned to our house the next evening, the night before the winner of the presidential election was announced in the States. He was a fixture in our humble home. Nothing out of the usual. He had told Anji he'd be over at 8:30 p.m., but he came early, at 7:15. Anji was out for a spa day, for which Mark had given her some money. Her skin wasn't as luminous as it had been before; among many things, she hadn't been sleeping well, she was restless. I'd hear her in the kitchen rattling around in the early mornings. On edge. Unsure. Moving *verry* funny.

We had four days remaining. Maybe we'd be given two days' grace before the landlord would throw us out on the street. Maybe I'd be struck by a truck, and my family could sue someone for all the money they'd ever need.

Tracey had offered we could stay with her. She had an extra bedroom and a sofa bed.

We didn't tell Mark that we faced eviction. We didn't tell a single one of our new friends. You know how people can be sometimes once they know that you're struggling. That look on their face. Any ounce of respect they may have had, squandered and down the drain. Even the kind and understanding didn't like to have their day ruined by another's pain, no?

Mark had come to our house that evening in a jolly mood, wearing a green sweater and new Levi's jeans. He ran straight to the kitchen with his briefcase, calling Maysha, Dilo, and me over to the kitchen table. He had Christmas lights hanging around his neck, running on batteries in a pack snug in his back pocket.

"Are you ladies ready?" He smiled, his hands on his briefcase.

The excitement. The thrill. We hovered behind his shoulders. Maysha squeezed right in and we waited, leaning closer in anticipation. Mark pinched the locks and pulled the buckles. He opened his briefcase, revealing stacks and stacks of money. Hundreds. Twenties. Fifties. More money than I'd ever seen in my lifetime. Maybe.

"Merry fucking Christmas, eh?" he whispered, making the sign of the cross.

"Praise the Lord!" I said, my hands raised high. I could hardly believe the sight before me.

Mark picked a bill from a stack.

"Here's twenty for May. Merry Christmas, sweetie."

Maysha grabbed the bill and blushed. She jumped up and down shrieking.

"I got million dollars!" that silly goose proclaimed.

Mark chuckled, embracing her. He rubbed his knuckles on her head.

"You think we should give Dilo a million dollars too, May?"

"No! Yes! Just a hundred . . . two hundred," said Maysha, with a hand on her hip and the facial expression of a middle-aged woman *verry* sure of herself. Ha! That girl softened our hearts. She reminded me much of our youngest sister, Kutti. At least, when Kutti was a child. It had been ten years since I'd last seen her.

Mark pulled another bill from a stack.

"That's twenty for this kid, right here," he said, handing Dilo twenty dollars, and then another five he pulled from his back pocket, he discreetly slipped into Dilo's hand. Really. Mark was considerate. Dilo was also happy.

"And now . . ."

Mark picked out another stack, hundred-dollar bills tied in a lime-green elastic. He began counting. Licking his thumb after every thousand.

"That's two thousand. Three. Four thousand. Five. Six, seven thousand dollars. Mary. I need you to tell Anji, this is for her brain. Keep this carefully, so Anji doesn't spend it on a new pair of . . . whatever she buys."

"Mark. Praise the Lord!" I held my brother's hand.

"That's seven thousand dollars? That's seven thousand dollars?" asked Dilo.

"Yeah, kid, you just saw me count it out." He half smiled and hit Dilo's shoulder. She hugged Mark. She smiled and quickly looked down at her feet.

"Thank you," she said.

"Don't sweat it," said Mark, turning round from Dilo, though he was pleased. He shut his briefcase, snapping the buckles in place.

"Shall I make some tea?" I asked, satisfied with all we

had been given so generously. But Mark put his hand on my shoulder. Those dimples!

"I have something very special for one of my *verry* favorite people," he said, and the girls gasped. They even giggled. Mark ran to the foyer, opened the front door, and carried in a box he must've left on the porch. He brought it straight to the kitchen.

"A juicer!" he shouted. Maysha hollered and squealed. "Think of all the smoothies you could be making, with all your fruits," said Mark gleefully, his arm around my shoulder.

What a glorious evening I shared with our girls.

I knelt against my bed and prayed. The door was shut, the curtains closed. The Tamil Radio played the sounds of a lone elephant. A bull in the night roaming through the jungle. Wolves howling in the thicket far in the distance. I pulled the suitcase from under my bed and placed the money, $7,000 in all, with my thaali and bracelets, wrapped in my father's hanky, kept in the folds of my silk Kanchipuram sari. I slid the juicer underneath as well, for another day. It was the first time, in a long time, I truly felt that we would be more than okay. The storm was passing.

At about 10 p.m. that same evening, Maysha and Dilo were on the carpet in front of the TV with bowls of popcorn. Tobias had recently dropped off a brand-new popcorn machine. Anji and I were on the couch under blankets holding cups of tea, with bowls of spicy cashews, fig biscuits, and grapes on the coffee table in front of us. Mark reclined on the easy chair, his briefcase against one side. He crossed his legs. Then uncrossed them. He ran his hands through his hair and he wiggled his toes in his socks.

The fridge was full, and our fruit bowl overflowed. The Tamil Radio, somehow always in tune with our moods, played Carnatic songs. Tharithajam for hours. I prayed for Mark. For his legs to calm from jittering. Every channel covered updates on the American election. The market, he feared, was unstable.

Mark reached for his BlackBerry from his back pocket, lifting his bum to one side. He pulled out his Ericsson phone from the holster clipped to his belt. He looked over at Anji and me on the love seat. He glanced down at his pager. He made a croaky sound as he lifted himself off the easy chair, grabbing his briefcase before making his way toward the kitchen. Anji and I shared a glance. Dilo turned round and said, "The guy thinks we'll take his money," and she laughed.

"Did Mark give you seven thousand dollars?" whispered Anji.

I nodded. Wondering about her doubt. I had heard the bathroom fan rushing, the door shutting. The click of the lock. All the while the Tamil Radio played those Carnatic tunes.

Thari tha jam, thari tha jam, thari tha

A few days before that night, a few days before the last return—before all this money came into our lives—Anji and Dilo were in the backyard. Maysha was asleep on the love seat beside me. One of Dilo's DVDs played—maybe, what was it, *Good Fellows* or something. Mark, who was lounging on the easy chair, turned my way and grinned.

"How come you don't want to invest with me anymore?" he asked.

"I have no money, darling." I laughed.

Mark smiled with his eyes this time.

"You don't have another bracelet or—"

"My thaali?"

He nodded.

"Oh, you must be crazy!" We laughed together, just the two of us.

I never mentioned that evening. I didn't think much of Mark asking his question; it seemed nothing out of the usual. He had an understanding of our situation. The first day he arrived, we only had the groceries he'd helped provide. The house wasn't as full as it warmed up to be after the Original Batch came into our lives and filled every corner of our home with kindness. Mark also had a hand in bringing us new friendships. But I told God what Mark had asked me and left it at His feet.

Days had passed; the memory was no bother. Suddenly, it was December 11. Mark was taking his time in the bathroom.

My mother had said I was born under the neem tree. I slithered from her arms and up the trunk into the branches, until my father called an elephant keeper to climb and fetch me. Can you imagine? In my first memory, I was four. I was scolded for dropping a bowl of prepared and sweetened butter fruit, leaving a pale green mess on the floor. My father had brought the butter fruit all the way from the Hill Country. Five kilos he bought from a woman who picked tea on the plantations. She had two giant trees across her family's line house planted by a British factory owner in 1930. From our kitchen I was propelled, as my mother shouted at the wastage. I sidewinded into the walls and out of our door, down the lane, hiding under a bench at the bus station. I remember the horror of people screaming. My father found me crouched in a bus shelter. He dragged me to the car, where he and my mother beat me.

I recall a time in 1964, when I was nine. Our family of six—my parents, myself, and my three siblings—were in Trincomalee for my chiththi's wedding. In the late evening at the bridal house, as nearly twenty of us gathered wrapping rich cake, in between the laughter and sharing of old stories, the wind whistled before thrashing. A corrugated roof flew past the front window. We ran to huddle in the bathroom; others raced to the servant's chamber. A cyclone was passing, rumbling over the roof until segments collapsed into the house, falling on the rug, hurtling to the floor. The furniture under the exposure crashed against the walls from the wind, shattering glass, tumbling trinkets, pieces of the home in shambles. *Chi!* I held Anji, who was one year old at the time, protecting her head, crouching in a small corner by the sink, covering her ears from the clank of destruction, the hollering of our cousins and the rest of our family. I passed Anji to a cousin-brother, feeling a sensation course throughout my body. Despite everyone's refusal, I ran out from the bathroom to the veranda, equally terrified and amazed by the devastation. The world before me pulled and dragged along as the wind thundered, and I serpentined up an arasamaram, coiling tightly on a branch, seeing other trees uprooting before my eyes, witness to the death of my chiththi's goats and cows and garden.

When I felt that tingle in my toes, the unnerving of my spirit, a fear for my life and those around me, my scales would form, and I knew it was best to seek refuge with the trees or call to my Lord and savior for His mercy. There was my ancestral calling, and there was my faith in my redeemer. *Chi!* What a life, no?

In 1988, Dilo was with Anji at our mother's house. Even if it had been a year since Jeevan was taken to be with the Lord, Anji was in need of healing. Aiyo! Aiyo! En theivamey! Lights dimming from our eyes. Entire lives changing from the loss of too many. How many gardens have we lost?

Anji's flight to Toronto was days away and she was most silent. She hadn't eaten in weeks. I worried for her life with us. And I worried for her life far from her family. She held Dilo tightly. In a room. In the dark. Dilo, unaware of her own chiththi's sadness, asked for her appa, in between each of Anji's sighs. For too many reasons, I felt an uncertainty that caught my breath, that pushed me down, that tingled in my toes to my fingers, up along my spine.

Kannan was hosting an ecological symposium and spent longer hours away, when he had already spent much time away from home. But that day, the dusty roads led me as my cobra, to find Kannan among colleagues, internationals and local professors, circled in the courtyard at the University of Jaffna. On the other side, the Tigers gathered in a disagreement with some members of faculty, opposite a wall dedicated to martyrs. Gone forever. Jeevan's face among many. On another side were photos of civilians. Uncles. Aunties. Somebody's children. Some child's amma and appa. The same. The same. The same.

I was coiled into the hollow of a silky oak tree, close to Kannan and his peers, when I heard my husband say loud and clearly, "There isn't much to say to a wife who believes the world was made in seven days and has no connection to history."

A white woman laughed, some pompous German professor with wide shoulders. I struck, biting her ankle. Feeling my fangs pierce her strawberry-thin skin, my venom rushing into her body. Swiftly I retreated and slithered far from campus, far from my own mother's house, up to the salt pans, close to Point Pedro.

My first and last bite. That pain and agony.

Ha! Really. What a life, no?

Mark stomped back into the living room and stood in front of the TV, appearing pale.

"You look like you just shit your pants, fam," said Dilo.

I threw a pillow at my child. Mark had his hand up. Anji muted the TV.

"Bobby's worried about the market right now. Sources say once the president is announced there's no telling what'll happen to the stock exchange."

He looked down at the carpet, behind the love seat, to the foyer.

"So, let's wait to make a trade with the five thousand. You don't want to take that risk, do you? You can still teach in a few days, though, can't you, Mark?"

Anji ran her fingers through her long black hair, which fell to one side.

"I'm supposed to teach the Five our trading course this Friday—"

"Yes, Mark, and you'll teach them on Friday, yes?"

"I've got more balls in this than you've got eggs. I know what I'm doing, all right?"

My eye began to twitch.

This one. The left one.

Twitching like this.

I needed oxygen. My skin began to itch. I had to rid myself of that terrible sensation. I went out for a walk in the cold and returned about an hour or so later. Dilo was in her room on the computer. Maysha was asleep on the carpet in front of the TV, popcorn scattered around her like snow. Mark and Anji conversed in a *verry* unpleasant way.

"I ran out of my car, and it slithered off in my yard," said Mark.

I crept straight to my room. Standing at my door, I knew someone had been in my bedroom. But my legs weakened from the knees. I couldn't even wash my face that night. I slipped off my clothes, shedding my skin in discomfort. I lay in my bed, seeing the ocean waves. Hearing the tide push and pull. Push and pull.

Kannan used to boast about our Miocene limestone when we'd walk along the coast in the north. I remembered so clearly. Our footprints in the sand.

"Miocene. Miocene. So what, then, is your creation story?"

I tumbled into dreams. I slithered over rocks and through paddy fields, through dusty roads into sheds, as the Tamil Radio played the songs of singing fish and mermaids bathing in the Eastern Lagoon. That night, I needed my rest.

Hustle Baby –

You think you'll ever get tired of playing checkers with me?

John Gotti –

I don't know

But do I make you horny, baby?

Hustle Baby –

Oh behave!

John Gotti –

LOL

Hustle Baby –

If you mix gasoline and frozen orange juice concentrate, do you know what you get?

John Gotti –

Napalm honey

LOL

Movies can change the world

Hustle Baby –

Don't call me honey

John Gotti –

Oh shit

My bad

Lol

Hustle Baby –

It's your turn

John Gotti –

Do I make you horny tho?

Hustle Baby –

Gotti . . .

John Gotti –

You make me hard

Just talking to you

I'd love to see a picture of you

Kinda weird I don't know what my gf looks like

I'm not some weirdo

I really really like you :(

Hustle Baby –

The internet is make-believe

John Gotti –

But we're real people

I'd pay money to see you in a bikini, HB

Just tell me how much you need

ACT 4

DILO

DECEMBER 12

Anji didn't sleep. I heard her banging on Mary's door at about one in the morning, maybe. Every time I woke up to pee, I saw her pacing the halls, the foyer, the whole house. And I got up to pee more than usual that night. I couldn't tell you why.

That morning breakfast was a waffle drenched in syrup made by yours truly, Chef Moi. I folded mine up like a taco. The December sky was bright, cerulean, and cloudless. The days had become shorter and colder, so there would be less time to make money. People shopped during the day; those looking for goods at night weren't typically interested in paying for them.

Anji's anklets jingled, alerting me that she was coming out of her room.

"Mary! Mary!"

It was eight in the morning. Mary and Maysha were at the table enjoying my waffles. Mary called in sick because—what she told me was that her head hurt from hardly sleeping. I had big plans for the day, and they involved skipping a few classes. Taking a break. A break. I could take a break, I thought.

"What the hell were you thinking last night, akka? And I was knocking on your door for hours."

"I took a sleeping pill. What do you want from me. Sit. Eat. Dilo made waffles. Tobias brought that waffle maker, no?"

"So good, Mommy!" said Maysha with syrup all over her face.

Anji pulled out a chair and sat directly in front of Mary.

"I know what you did. He wet his pants even," she whispered.

"Who pissed themselves?" I asked with a mouthful of waffle.

"*Chi!* Close your mouth, pillai. Eat some fruit. Did you eat any fruit? You didn't eat fruit yesterday, did you?"

"Akka. I said something important."

"Enna-di?"

"Mark came back to our house after he left."

"And did you give him new pants to wear?" asked Mary.

"He was terrified, you fool! What were you thinking? He's already a basket case!"

"Basket what?"

"Why did you do it?"

"I left something in his car, di. He came at the wrong time. Leave it. I didn't go to work because of a headache and now you are causing more harm. *Chi.* I really hope you gave him a pair of pants to wear."

Anji huffed and stormed back to her room, knowing herself enough to know that she was a monster if she hadn't slept.

After clearing the table and messing around knowing we had twenty dollars each to spend at Z-Mart later, Maysha and I were seated with the cordless and the phone book, prank calling whatever number Maysha's little finger landed on, her alphabet book conveniently positioned between us. We heard Anji's anklets and shut the phone book quick.

"Nine forty-five. He's not coming back."

"What?"

"Mark. Did he call?"

I shook my head.

"Were you on the phone? Did you hear another line?"

I shook my head again.

Anji laughed, and her eyes said, *Imma beat that boy with my slipper.*

That afternoon we all gathered around the TV to watch Mary and Anji's favorite soap, *Days of Our Lives.* It was mindless, but it helped ease the tension just a tiny bit. A welcome distraction from the news that the election in the "free world" had been stolen. Though Anji had said democracy was a "tool used to placate society."

"Do you think Mark is okay?" asked Mary during a commercial break.

"If he's not dead, I'll kill him myself," answered Anji sternly.

"You guys are gonna pay the landlord the entire seven

thousand, right? So, we don't have to worry so much till February," I said.

"We have expenses, Dilo. Akka, Mark gave you the money. He gave you that money, yes?"

Mary's face dropped. Her mouth opened. She froze, not even blinking. Sometimes my mother put reality on the back burner and forgot the burner was still on. She scurried to her bedroom. Anji followed after, only making it to the kitchen, where she stumbled and held the wall for support. I fetched a glass of water for her, afraid she would collapse. Maysha fanned her mother with the alphabet book, guiding her to sit down.

The maple tree in the backyard looked shriveled in the winter air. A thin layer of ice caught the afternoon light, turning the yard a chilly gray.

A shriek from Mary's bedroom.

"My gold! Our seven thousand. It's gone! All gone!" she repeated weakly.

I sped down the hallway, almost tripping over my socks. I found Mary in a heap on the carpet, her suitcase wide open beside her. The smell of my appa wafted through the room. My grandfather's hanky. Our yellowed landing documents. Mothballs and lavender. Red kumkum in a pot, and the musty aroma from Mary's Kanchipuram sari. Her finest silk sari.

DECEMBER 13

Anji refused to leave her room that morning. I was forced to care for Maysha longer than usual. We spent most of our day trying to coax our mothers back to health. Mary had called out of work sick, again, due to a debilitating migraine. I didn't step foot out the front door. We had two days to come up with the money, but it seemed like everyone else had already given up. Worn out. Broken.

Five p.m. and still no word from Mark. He'd normally call when the stock market closed at four every afternoon, if he wasn't already in our home. We only knew him for a month and a half, but it had felt like a lifetime. He felt like a member of our family. We'd shared so much together. The food, the snacks, the movies. I couldn't believe I actually missed that waste man; we all did. Maysha even cried, she missed him so much.

We told the Original Batch not to come over. They usually came by after they finished their shifts. Trickling in off the 401, sometimes early enough to get bits of dinner with us. We told the Five the same story. We had contracted a terrible stomach bug, and we were all shitting our pants and throwing up our brains.

Mary retreated even further into her faith, shouting out Bible verses in both English and Tamil. Reminded me to read Psalm 91. She begged us to pray with her. I whispered a tiny prayer. Maysha and I were bussing cups of tea in and out of both bedrooms for most of the day. When Anji and Mary tired of drinking cups of tea, they switched to rum. A bottle open on the table.

"What do you think?" asked Mary.

"I can't even think," said Anji.

We didn't say much to each other.

DECEMBER 14

Mary went to work that morning. I spent my time between classes—skipped only two—at the Malvern Mall, at Z-Mart. Anywhere I could find people. Asking around. Looking for action. Hoping for an opportunity.

I sold the gloves off my hands for two dollars. Was enough to buy Maysha takeout for dinner.

It was 7 p.m. Leon left a plate of cevapi on the porch. Nelly left two jars of pea soup. Mary and Anji were still seated by the kitchen table, waiting for Mark to return and save the day. Tracey wanted to come over, but I told her it wasn't a good time. If depression had a smell, I knew its every particle. Half a pomegranate left carelessly on the cutting board, unseeded. The edges of the fruit beginning to shrivel. The other half lazily cut and abandoned in a dirty bowl. Pith still encased around too many neglected seeds. Maysha watched *Rambo* in the living room. Between the television and the Tamil Radio, our home sounded like a war zone. Whizzing arrows and flying bullets.

"Maybe he had a heart attack? Mark enjoyed the fast food, no?"

Anji didn't respond.

"He would've called. He always calls. What about the training? My friend Sheila and her friends."

Anji poured herself another glass of rum. She relit her rollie, staring off into nowhere in particular. Someplace better than here.

"Sheila must be preparing a feast for the training... Mark will come, no? He must be sick. The weather changed too fast too soon. Everyone was blowing their nose on the bus."

Anji had printed twenty booklets titled *Trade Today, Be Your Own Boss Forever*. She reappropriated bits and pieces of information Mark had been able to scrape off the internet, filled with corny stock jargon and cheesy puns. *The Trend Is Your Friend! Don't Be Late, Anticipate to Be Great! The Sun Rises Every Day, So Should Your Portfolio! Work Smarter, Fart Harder!* Malarkey. Trash. Empty words, for hungry people.

She poured a lot of time into the layout and construction of this scheme with graphs and pie charts, and I should know, because I was kept out of my room. Off the computer. Disconnected. The booklets were stacked up on the kitchen counter; she'd even gotten them bound professionally.

"He could call tonight," said Anji, straight-faced and staring at the wall.

"You think he'll call tonight? You really think so?" asked Mary.

And then, the phone rang.

Rrrrrring
Rrrrrring

"Who is it?" Anji asked me.

I read the display.

"Private Caller."

Anji stood from her chair. Mary held her heart, blowing a kiss at her portrait of Jesus.

"Hello?... Sheila. Praise the Lord... yes, we're all feeling much better, thanks. Mark ordered us some fish and chips, and you know how fish gets . . . Great, you have a caterer set up for tomorrow, but I'm afraid we'll have to postpone, dear. Mark may have cancer, Sister Sheila... I know, everyone is getting cancer these days. It's a terrible thing. I really appreciate you being so understanding . . . We're hopeful and praying. That's all we can do... Yes, we're still waiting for his results . . . I should get going, I'm– Thank you, sister. I will. Praise the Lord. Thank you... Bye."

Anji put the receiver down. The TV stopped. The Tamil Radio was silent for once. Anji opened the utility drawer. She pulled out a paring knife. She walked to the cutting board and steadied herself, placing one hand on the counter. She took a breath in and then stabbed the pomegranate repeatedly.

Ta. Ta. TA. TA. TA.

Juice spurted on the counter, on the backsplash, on the cabinet doors. But she wouldn't stop.

Ta. Ta. TA. TA. TA.

Red splattered on her face, on her hands, on my skin.

"That rat! That cowardly son of a bitch!"

Anji put the knife down and wiped it with a kitchen towel. She placed the knife back in the drawer before pulling out her silver smoke tin. She got herself another rollie and walked to the foyer. She slipped on her boots, put on her trench, and walked out the front door into that cold December evening.

Hustle Baby –

You busy?

Ur taking a long time to move

John Gotti –

Sorry. Just dealing with something

Hustle Baby –

What happened?

You haven't really been urself

John Gotti –

I played checkers with you yesterday

And we're playing right now

Hustle Baby –

But you haven't been messaging the same

I don't know

Sowwie

John Gotti –

Fuck HB!

I got a lot going on

These girls keep sending me pics of them 2

Hustle Baby –

Random girls?

John Gotti –

Girls I'm talking 2

Just friends

Obviously!

Hustle Baby –

They might be sending viruses
tho

John Gotti –

No viruses

Just pics of hot girls in bikinis

Its fine

Hustle Baby –

Oh you opened them already

John Gotti –

Yeah

I can't look at hot pics now?

Hustle Baby –

You can do whatever you want

I just don't like being a gf

John Gotti –

Oh come on!

Don't be a prude

Don't chicken out

Shit!

TTYL

Got a business call

I love you

ANJI

That bugger! That bloody guy! Just like that—he was gone. Houdini! That shit bag!

Mark walked out of our door with $82,460 in his briefcase. Every bill of which I counted by hand. Ten grand from each of the Five; that was $50,000. Three thousand from the Original Batch, combined. And then I have to give Mark some credit, he somehow convinced Sister Sheila to give him the cash for a down payment for a property on Sixteenth Avenue with Sebastian, Mark's "Realtor friend," a whopping $29,500 *in cash.* A total of $82,500 minus $40 he shared with Dilo and Maysha. To think of the efforts he made to take back our $7,000; the desire to give and then take right away.

I thought if he was going to bail, he would at least have the decency to wait *a couple of days* after having received the money. At least try to make it seem like he was legitimate, lull us into a sense of security, before jetting off into the ether with the money. Maybe after a day of training with the Five to get them off our backs. Maybe come up with his own elaborate story using the trust he gained with Sister Sheila as leverage to weasel even more from another few trades. Although it was all based on a lie, we had built a real community. Mark owed us all that. Hell, he owed me everything he had. Make us all *feel* good, before ruining our lives. He was more cruel than cunning. He was pathetic. No, I was pathetic. I thought I was good, but Mark proved better. That wasn't easy to admit to myself.

The plan was for me to hang on to the $25,000 that was designated for trading. Mark was meant to deposit the amount in my account. He refused to keep that much in our house because we lived in Malvern, and he bought into all the stories. Mark would keep the money for the cost of his training program, and he told the Five that after the training, if they weren't satisfied with their learning, he would return their money no questions asked. I plotted to pilfer that stash. Perhaps have Dilo get one of her friends to fake a mugging.

A thief in the night. He took it all! Our gold! And the $7,000 he'd handed over that evening. What was I thinking? What was I going to tell everyone? I couldn't possibly tell anyone the truth. We were too close, too involved.

I always knew there was a chance Mark could cheat me, I just didn't think he had the audacity. To do something so terrible to Tobias? To Reina? To Mary? The men had started a bowling team; they were a unit of their own. Foolishly, I hoped that if his returns were a scam, I'd be in on the deal, that I could steer the fraud in the right direction. It mattered who was conned, and for what reason. Ninety-nine percent of the world didn't deserve to suffer. They just needed something of their own, something to give them purpose and meaning.

Mark and I had watched each other. I thought he assumed we were on the same page. I caught his eyes on me in every room. At church. When he pitched potential investors, or even when he traded on his own. As if to say, *Can you believe they're buying my bullshit?* But for me to assume, how foolish. I played him in every interaction. I myself was never honest.

What was most crucial, what I kept to myself for some time: I believed Mark didn't intend to leave so abruptly. If he made a plan of escape, if the intention was to scam us all eventually, I don't think he had scheduled our betrayal for that Tuesday morning. The night before, on Monday, December 11, Mark came back to our house after having said goodbye. He came to our house with his briefcase.

"Oh my God. You look terrible. That smell—"

I had opened the front door, seeing it was Mark's car that pulled up to our driveway. His face was pallid and dull. His jeans appeared dark around the crotch and down his inner thigh.

"There was a snake in my car." He shivered, pushing himself through the door and walking straight to the kitchen.

"What do you mean, there was a snake in your car?"

"There was a fucking cobra in my BMW, and it slithered from the back to the front and on my lap when I parked in my driveway."

"How do you know it wasn't a viper?"

"Are you kidding me?"

"I'm just surprised you know what a cobra is, it's a very specific accusation."

"I've seen fucking *Aladdin,* Anji! Do you think you're the only cultured person in this room?"

He stumbled to the sink and ran the tap. He opened his mouth to catch the water and slurped, allowing the stream to wet his mouth and cheeks, before falling backward toward a chair at the kitchen table.

"I think I'm having a stroke—"

"Are you okay, Mark?"

"I said, I think I'm having a stroke! You're really not listening to me."

"Sit down. Take a breath," I instructed, helping him into the chair.

I rubbed his sweaty head and put the kettle on. I put two slices of bread in the toaster.

"It was on my lap, Anji . . . It slithered onto my lap, and its black tongue was this close to stabbing me up the nostril. Am I dreaming? Please tell me I'm dreaming. I gotta be fucking dreaming or I've been drugged. Tobias could've had some meth in that popcorn maker. Fuck! Tell me something, hooker! Tell me something now!"

"Mark."

"Don't look at me like that. What? What, Anji? What?"

"Do you think that was the devil? The devil was in your car, maybe? Jesus Christ, do you think it was the devil, Mark?"

I threw two tea bags in a pot while the water boiled in the kettle.

"I didn't pray yesterday—"

His voice sullen, his head down.

"Are you doing something God wouldn't approve of, Mark? Are you doing something *bad*?"

I scraped a dried curry splatter off the counter with the back of a spoon, my eyes out toward the backyard.

I gave him a glass of water. I handed him a plate of buttered toast with brown sugar sprinkled on top. I poured us two glasses of black tea once it was perfectly steeped. We sat dipping the toast in our cups. Mark sighed when he finished. He pushed back his chair and brushed his shirt clean of any crumbs.

"I'll see you tomorrow. Before ten. Twelve at the latest. If you don't hear from me—I'm dead."

The one true thing he ever said to me. He went to the bathroom, washed his face, and then headed out the door, having slipped his sneakers on. He didn't turn back. Not even a glance. Just like that, Mark walked out. I didn't think for a second I'd never see him again.

John Gotti –

You get my message?

Hustle Baby –

The American Psycho business card template?

Yeah

Thank you :)

John Gotti –

I know you got your own cards – but this was a file worth downloading

I got something at Wal-Mart for U 2

Just gotta know where to send it

Hustle Baby –

What is it?

John Gotti –

Some lingerie . . .

I got a few gifts for you

Hustle Baby –

I have my own stuff

John Gotti –

Shit

Hustle Baby –

What?

John Gotti –

My ex

She sent me something

Hustle Baby –

What is it?

John Gotti –

Damn . . .

Hustle Baby –

What?

John Gotti –

Just her at the beach on my old jet ski

Her ass is out lol

Hustle Baby –

Are you going to delete it?

John Gotti –

Listen HB

You can't tell me what to do

Not like uv ever sent anything 2 me

. . . maybe we shouldn't do this NE more

Hustle Baby –

I just asked you a question

John Gotti –

I can't do jealous girls, HB

Hustle Baby –

I'm not jealous

John Gotti –

Sure

I love ya, but . . .

Hustle Baby –

I was going to send you a picture of me

John Gotti –

Really? . . .

Hustle Baby –

Yeah

Wearing these cool pants I got

John Gotti –

Without a top on?

Jk ;)

Hustle Baby –

Would you really pay me?

John Gotti –

If it's sexy!

Hell yeah!

I just melted tho fo real

I can't wait to see, HB

Attach File

Send

Delivered: 11:58 p.m.

MARY

I believed in prayer, not medication, but my sister needed a brain transplant. She could've done better with the heart of a pig. I began to believe that maybe she had lied about accepting Christ as her personal Lord and savior. *Chi.* The only faith that woman had was in disaster. She didn't even have faith in herself. What I would do if I had half her looks, half her talent, half her brain. I would be a millionaire. Anji's main problem was that she could not see how life was a test, and our purpose was to prove our love and faith in the Lord. Glory be to His name.

DECEMBER 14

I had one thing on my mind, and that thing was pronounced "rent." Anji barged into the house, passed the living room, not even stopping to greet her baby Maysha. She stormed into the bathroom, slamming the door behind her.

"Anji. Anji. Get out from there, please. You've been a drama queen the whole day. Please, Maysha is crying, di."

I hit the door with my palms and waited. And waited. I had been waiting for days. I had been waiting for months. I had been waiting for years. My trust was in the Lord, who has not failed me. Joshua 1:9.

"Have I not commanded thee? Be strong and of a good courage. Be not afraid . . ."

"Anji, open the door. Please. Maysha has fallen and broken her leg."

Dilo was on the computer. The blue light shone from under the door. The house might have been falling to pieces and that girl wouldn't have moved an inch from that chair. Since the computer entered our house, nothing had ever been the same.

No matter what I said, Anji would not leave the bathroom. There was only one thing left to try.

"I know where he lives, Anji. Thirty-Four Cherry Wood Lane. You're wasting time."

Dilo poked her head out from her room, still hiding in the darkness. My sister, my sweet thangachchi. From under the bathroom door, I saw as her shadow moved closer. The doorknob began to twist.

It was dark outside, that early morning. Racoon families on missions to destroy people's driveways and flower beds. Thieves and rapists and sinners drank liquor in alleyways. This was the devil's time, no?

"Tracey trusted you with her car this late?"

"Please, I can't talk while I'm driving, Anji."

"Jesus, akka. I could drive and you can navigate. It's not a problem. Stop over there—"

"You don't even take the garbage out on Tuesday nights when I ask, do you think I can trust you with my directions?"

"I take the garbage out most weeks. How close does he live? Don't tell me he's been within walking distance this whole—"

"Anji, I'm driving and it's dark. *Chi.* I didn't bring my glasses."

"Just park over there for a second. I need to know."

My sister was a number 8. I was a Christian, so I didn't follow Tamil numerology, but number 8s were children of Saturn, and Saturn would never let go of her rings. Struggling, I still managed. I found a safe spot along a curb.

"What is it, vesi, this is not a good time."

"Why did you follow him? Akka, please. Stop fiddling with the seat cover, I asked you something."

"We never asked him enough about his living situation."

"He said his house was under renovation."

I let Anji's voice remain in the car so she could hear the words she said. The night was quiet. Children were sleeping. I worried about Dilo on the computer late at night. In that stillness, I felt fear fiercely rattling in my ear.

“We had plenty on our minds,” said Anji, her shoulders dropping.

“I was curious, Anji. Something wasn’t right; you know I get that feeling. The Lord guides me, no?”

“If you want to call it your Lord, sure. But why didn’t you tell me?”

“What? Give you Mark’s address that night? For what purpose?”

She sighed, rubbing her thighs. She relaxed into the seat and sighed again. And again.

“He would’ve stolen the money that night.”

“Did you see him go in my bedroom when he came back smelling of urine?”

She was quiet. She ran her finger along the window, through the condensation. That fog.

“Could you not sense that he went in your room?” she asked.

I put the car back into drive and steered from the curb back onto the road, in the right direction.

“Akka, did you not know?”

“Anji, listen to me. I was tired. I am tired. Let me just pray while I drive.”

We were silent for the rest of the ten-minute drive. Anji was karuavaadu. Dried fish in a parka. I’d only managed so far because I had God. Holding the wheel. Holding my hands. Keeping me tight on His lap that night. I drove and I drove, and I trusted Him. I was worried about Mark, too. I was *verry* worried for him. He was my main concern, actually. Imagine what he would be feeling. I prayed for him. In my spirit, I knew, something terrible would find that boy, if it hadn't already. Dragged in a ditch. Beaten by the bank machine. I put a worship tape in the cassette player.

> *. . . whatever my lot, thou hast taught me to say*
> *It is well*
> *It is well with my soul.*

I saw a tear close to falling from the middle of Anji's left eye. The streetlights lit that single tear on her beautiful skin, her beautiful face. Our mother's cheeks. Our mother's pride. Our father's color. Anji swiftly caught the drop with her finger. She dragged it across her temple and rubbed the sadness through her hair, pulling the trouble down to her ear and along her jaw.

ANJI

Boxwood barricaded the lawn and wrapped round the bungalow. Stacks of wooden two-by-fours were piled in a corner. The temperature had dropped that night and I wasn't dressed for the weather. The forecast warned it could snow.

From the outside, the house looked abandoned. The brick was dull, the gutters heavy; the trash bin at the back of the driveway was full and bursting at the brim. Neither his "new" BMW nor his '95 Ford Escort was in sight.

"Shall we go back now?" asked Mary, fiddling with the rearview mirror.

"Did you think you were going to show me where Mark lives and that would be the end of it?" I asked, opening the door.

"I thought we could pray for Mark in the car."

I stepped out from the passenger side and grabbed the tire iron under the seat. Of course, our friend Tracey's car was equipped in case of an attack. I slipped the iron into my parka.

The premises were secure. The neighbors asleep, and elderly. Extra rails on the porch. Disabled sticker on their car. Retired and in bed. Hopefully, hard of hearing.

The window at the side of the house was far too high for me to reach. There was a separate entrance to the basement, but I couldn't have picked that lock. I climbed over the back gate, avoiding the betrayal of a squeaky hinge. He had a sliding back door, which he may have left unlocked.

I hit the glass. Twice. It felt good to bash it in. Twinkling stars crashing down on dingy cement blocks. Minding my pants on any sharp edges, I was in.

His living room was in complete disarray. Heavily worn and torn floral furniture, half missing cushions. A smattering of family photos on the mantel. Striped wallpaper peeled at the corners. A basket of yarn on the floor. Empty cans of beer littering the carpet. I could smell only the stench of his mess. A damp towel drying on a dead radiator. His dirty clothes. His sweaty socks.

I had little time. The clock on the mantel a reminder I needed to be quick.

Tick
Tick
Tick

There was an open door in the hallway, which led into the kitchen. On the table was a bag of bread, a plate of butter, a dirty knife, and a Nail Gun Pro. The sink overflowed with an assortment of used plates and bowls. I smelled rotting food in a pool of water.

Through the kitchen was a doorway that led to the basement. I could hear someone in the shower. Water dripping off a body.

Tick
Tick

Down the rotted steps and into the creepy cellar. A safe and secluded space suitable for a troll. A lava lamp, blue headlights, and a pair of subwoofers. A pubescent boy's movie posters covered one wall. Tarantino, *The Godfather, The Mask*. Another wall plastered with image after image of breasts. Wet breasts. Fake breasts. Wet-and-wild-on-spring-break breasts. The shower continued running. The troll unaware he had guests.

On the desk were two monitors, his computer, and a phone. The computer was still on. The sound of its systems in operation. The light pulling me closer.

I minimized the graphs. It was the brightest screen I'd ever seen, forcing me to squint my eyes. A warning.

Look the other way, foolish woman. Leave with your peace. Go home.

The desktop was the most organized thing in his house. A folder stood out in all capital letters. "HELLO." I clicked through a series of folders—like nesting dolls—until I reached one titled "Girls."

Tick
Tick
Tick

Aisha . . . Amanda . . . Cindy . . . Erika . . . Reina, of course. I rolled my eyes. And then an unexpected familiar name. One I knew from somewhere, near and too close to my everything.

I double-clicked.

The water stopped running. Stopped dripping and falling. Stopped rushing warm on a body incapable of ridding itself of filth. I didn't have enough time to look for what I hoped to find. I didn't have time to think. I ran upstairs with even more questions, questions that I would never have answers for.

I saw what I saw.

If some people died, the world would be a much better place.

DILO

Where are you? Did you not receive my messages? Did you find another box? You said mine made your heart beat a little faster. You said mine was the most fun. Was it the shape of me? Was it my color? I thought I lightened the pictures enough. I played with the exposure, but maybe that was too much.

Did I say something wrong? Was I too annoying? Did I send back one smiley face too many? Did you find someone more steaming hot than I'd ever be, who lived closer? Did she send you a picture of the inside of her butt?

Did I do something wrong? Say something stupid? Was I a pest? A bug? A fly that buzzed around your face for too long?

. . .

What did I do to be left alone without a goodbye, or simply a "That was nice, you take care now," or "I had a good time talking to you." Or "Have a wonderful life. Got to go."

I would've been perfectly all right with that.

Millions and millions of people. Millions and millions of profiles.

You said my box was special. The most special box was mine.

Hustle Baby –

Hey Gotti?

Are you there?

It was 1 a.m. I was plugged in and online. I assumed Mary and Anji were still out on their mission. I wasn't in the mood to tag along, as much as I enjoyed a night ride. Plus, Maysha was asleep in front of the TV. I did all I could to clear my mind, my stomach upside down and churning. I checked out my favorite websites. Some stop-motion animation made using Paint by a kid from Colorado. A Tennessee man's swamp property photography. I read about the 160 asylum seekers feared drowned off the coast of Australia. I read about the newly elected US president's plans for the economy. I read articles on Teen-y Women about how a boob job could increase a woman's rate of success, and a how-to on kissing a boy while on your period so he doesn't smell fish and hate you. I read up on the Sudbury crater, which usually made me feel "small" and "insignificant" in the best of ways. I played Tetris. Offline.

What troubled me so much that I couldn't sleep? Just that we had to pay rent in a few hours, and I hadn't even found a buyer for our TV or DVD player. I couldn't sell a thing. My supplier had bailed on me, ever since Ms. Lieberman shut down my operation. I'd promised Mary I'd figure something out. But I was tired. Mark had taken money from our family. I had enough to be pissed about, and to top it off, I had a headache.

I heard her anklets first. Didn't hear the car pull up to the driveway. Didn't hear Mary. Didn't hear Maysha wake up or nothing. The hallway light filled my room as Anji swung the door wide open, before charging straight for me. She shook me by the shoulders. One hand held me down, the other gripped my neck. Choking. Choking me. Anji's eyes were bloodshot. Anji's eyes screamed.

I didn't know what I did wrong. I didn't know if I'd made a terrible mistake. If I hurt her, or our family, or cost us some cash, or tarnished my grandfather's name. I didn't know if I was being sent to jail or deported. I didn't know what was going on.

Her nostrils flared and her lip quivered. Her face contorted. Her grip grew incrementally tighter around my throat. A slow release. My hands holding her arms—tearing at the one holding me down. Prying at the one clasping my neck. Trying to remember my internet-tutorial-learned survival strategies and grappling techniques. Attack the thumb. I tried and I tried, but she overpowered me. My thoughts began to cloud.

I was laid out, under a maple tree surrounded by a hundred milkweed blossoms. Wild columbine dangled over me, tickling my nose. I was the meadow bluestem. I was the tall grass in the wind. I was a lone little insect. I was free again. I ran through the field surrounded by goldenrod and cattails and bullfrogs croaking. Croaking. My throat. My air. A hole filled with dirt.

"You vesi!

"You foolish girl.

"You never listen.

"You'll never learn.

"You could've been raped!

"You could've gotten yourself killed!"

She let go of my neck. We would speak nothing of this, ever again.

I feared there was a clot of blood I had to pass from out of my mouth. Stuck in my throat. My neck burned. Burned. Burned.

"Right there. You don't see it? You never once looked up and read what that says? What does the sign say, Dilo? What does it say? Read it, damn it!"

"'Don't talk to strangers. Don't talk to strange men—'" I struggled.

My voice hoarse and soft.

"And you went and put on my underwear?"

"What?"

"You put on my underwear in your disgusting pictures, you vesi. My push-up bra. My lace—you did that!"

"What are you talking about?"

"Did you and Mark do anything in this house?" she asked, her voice trembling. Her hands shaking.

"What?"

"Answer me."

"What? Mark? What's going on?"

"You're going to take a pregnancy test. You're going to take a test."

"What?"

"You stupid girl!"

She slapped me. She beat me. She beat me again and again, all over. Bruising my skin. Mary may have been praying in her room. Maybe she had taken some sleeping pills again. Maybe she was at Tracey's. Mother Mary didn't come for me, but Maysha was at my door. I saw her as Anji beat me. I saw her through the hair that fell over my face as I crouched to protect my body. My body. My ugly dirty body.

"Mommy?" called Maysha.

Anji put her hands down. Her face flushed red. Knuckles swollen. Palms probably stinging. Anji fell on the carpet. She pulled her hair. She hit her head. Maysha looked at me for a reaction. I didn't have one. Looking glumly at my feet. The hole in my sock. My big toe sticking out. Everything just dirty.

Maysha walked over to her mother. She gave Anji a hug.

"Don't do that, Mommy. You know hitting not okay."

That white dog with the spot round its eye was in my drawer. I couldn't feel nothing no more. I gave Maysha the dog. She smiled and kissed the dog's tummy.

The night was dark. Or was it the early morning. The ground was cold on my palms.

When I close my eyes, I am in a clock tower, and this is where I live with a garland of jacaranda around me.

There is a light, and it calls my name.

"Child, sweet child, one day you will follow, but you can't come up here now. You're not supposed to die today. You got to feel some more, pillai. You got to pain some more, joy some more, love some more, and smile some more, before you are a spore again. Don't follow the light, little one. Don't follow the light."

What was just if you were born into a world where children died by a bullet to their head?

That world was yours.

And yours.

And yours.

Fuck those animals. Fuck those whores. Fuck this disgusting culture. I was slave to the earth. I was nothing. I was dirt. I will be gone.

Thou shalt not be afraid for the terror by night; nor for the arrow that flieth by day, I whispered Psalm 91 verse 5 to myself.

"Dilo?"

His face in a new location. His voice. I never thought about how it might sound in real life.

"So, you're coming over here like it's Disneyland, eh? How do you know where I live? Were you the one who broke my sliding door? Never mind. Come in. It's cold outside."

He looked out to see if I was alone. If anyone was with me. He seemed unbothered. Not as surprised as I expected. I slipped to the side, cornering him. I had the advantage of space. He shut the door.

"Where the hell have you been, asshole? Who the fuck do you think you are? You think I don't notice how often you quote *Heat*?" I growled.

"What? Don't talk to me like that, kid. I'm dealing with a break-in right now. I don't have time for a teenage meltdown. The cops should be here any minute. I'm serious, all right. This is not a good time, Dilo."

"Sit your ass on the ground."

"Excuse me?" He laughed.

"I said sit, asshole. You heard me."

"You didn't bring your machete, did you? This has to be some kinda fucking joke!" He laughed some more.

"Sit your ass on the ground," I said, my voice shaking.

He raised his hands, his back to the wall. He slid. Sneering.

Beside him was a table with a big ugly vase. The vase wasn't too heavy in my grip. In my hands.

"I'm on house arrest, all right? Something happened and I can't leave the house. I can't use my phone. You know how the cops are, Dilo. Come on, let's sit at the table. You want a hot chocolate or something? You want a regular type of life?" He smirked.

I hit Mark in the head with the vase. Chunks of porcelain fell to the floor, shattering on impact. Dust on his face. In between his eyelashes, in his hair.

"Whaddya want from me?" he hollered.

I kicked him in the ribs. I could feel his body under my boot.

"You're not Al Pacino, asshole. You're not a fucking gangster either."

"What the hell? What are you talking about? Why are you here? Why are you acting like a psychopath?" he groaned, almost still laughing. "I don't want to hurt you, Dilo."

"Hurt me? You're the one on the ground, you sick fuck!"

"Oh, come on. Let's talk, all right. I'm not in a good place right—"

"What's so funny?"

I crouched and held a piece of porcelain above his cheek. If he moved, I would slice him.

"Dilo! Come on. Let's be rational. You look really cute when you're angry. Of course I'm gonna smile."

My jaw dropped and I let out a sound. I screamed. I lost

something that night. Gone. Out the window. Something I'd never get back again. I stood, backing away, still pointing the porcelain in his direction. Eyes locked ahead. Ready for him to move even a single inch. He sat where he was. Watching me. Thinking this was a game. My life a game. Just something to play with.

I bumped into a table. A nail gun clattered to the floor. He sat up against the wall, eyes a little wider. I scanned the room to see if anyone else was home. The floor creaked. I looked back, and he was gone. He must've taken off down the hall. I grabbed the nail gun. Unlocked the safety. Checked if it was loaded. Back against the wall, I stalked my predator.

"Dilo—"

His voice.

"This isn't about the money, is it?"

His breathing. Labored from the bludgeoning of my boots.

"You could just tell me what you're upset about. We could talk. Just you and me. Like civilized adults."

His stench.

I held my breath. I was closer than he thought I was. Always lead with your weapon. I pointed the nail gun round the corner.

Pew

A nail ricocheted off the wall. He ducked. He didn't have to. He laughed. The nail tumbled to the floor.

"This isn't funny, Dilo," he said.

Pew

He held his arm.

"Fuck!"

His skin, red around the head of the nail that pierced his biceps. Now he was the one backing up.

"And, why in God's name would you do that?"

Pew

He held his shin.

"Damn it, Dilo. Fuck!"

"You know what you did. Just tell me why you did it. Why would you do that to me?"

Pew

He held his collar. He moaned in agony. Curling into a ball. His whimpers were intoxicating.

"Please stop," he said, struggling.

He banged the wall with his fist. In pain. I held the nail gun up at him. He held his hands up in surrender.

"It's funny—" he started. Sweat dripped down his forehead. I'd never seen this version of him. His true self and my friend John Gotti.

"You know how you said the one thing you wanted before the raptor was to have your first kiss?" he asked, looking at the wall, unable to look me in my eyes.

My arms were trying not to shake. The acid in my stomach shot up to my heart. My ribs squeezed my lungs too hard. I still had the nail gun aimed at his head. I wasn't seeing red anymore. I was seeing purple. Some blue. Some black. Some white light.

"What if the raptor was tomorrow? What if Jesus comes back by the time you're home, kid? You want to waste your life angry at me? I meant everything I ever said, HB."

His voice trembled. The pain he felt for me. His body riddled with nails.

Holey, holey, holey
This being before me
Broken in three persons
Tragic Trinity

The nail gun was heavy. My knees were shaking. My head spinning. My resolve failing. He didn't move any closer, but he held his hand out instead. I was falling.

"You wanna see my monkey?" he asked.

I didn't speak. Couldn't. I was on the floor. Beside him. Close enough.

He stuck his tongue behind his upper lip. He tugged on both his ears and made his eyes cross, looking down at the tip of his nose. Harmless.

He smiled, holding his chest. I was still crouched with the gun pointing at him, so close to him I could smell the strawberry sweets and tobacco on his breath.

"There's no winning out there, kid. Go ahead, shoot me

some more. You know I was real with you. You know I think you're special."

Pew
Pew

"How could you leave me, Gotti, without even saying goodbye?"

His grin. His laugh as he moaned in agony. He smiled at me and held his hand out. He pointed to his lips.

"Open your fucking eyes," I said, gritting my teeth. Shaking inside. Eyes welling up. "Wanna see me put nine-inch nails into each one of your eyelids?" The gun pointed right at him. My breathing, heavy.

He smirked. He smiled. I noticed, just then, Mark had two dimples.

Pew
Pew

MARY

The morning of December 15 was here at last. I was ready to pack our bags. I asked my manager for the day off. We had enough garbage bags for our things. I'd go to Z-Mart, later, to pick up some boxes. Tracey said we could keep the car for the day. This would not be the first time we had to grab our belongings on short notice.

Still, I had my faith. My God had fed five thousand with five loaves and two fish. My God had raised Lazarus from the dead. I was not afraid. Whatever storm, whatever tribulation, I was ready.

I walked down our hallway one last time, praising my God, as I turned the corner to enter the kitchen. I was met by a miracle: Mark's briefcase, right there on the kitchen table. Beside my father's hanky. My gold bracelets. My thaali.

I saw Anji outside smoking a cigarette through the sliding door. Dilo sat on the floor against the fridge, her skin ashy and dry. Her face. Something wasn't right with my girl. She'd never say. Only that her period had arrived. In our family, menstruation was more than cramps and aches. So, I let Dilo be. Maysha was in the living room playing with her dollies.

"Who brought this here?" I asked.

"I thought it was you," said Anji, coming in from outside.

"When did I go back to Mark's house?"

"Don't you ever say that name in this house again, akka."

"Vesi, this is about rent! Not your love story. Take it easy."

I turned to Dilo once more.

"Did you bring the briefcase here?"

She didn't move. I asked again. But she ignored me. These children were not afraid enough. This country had spoiled them.

"Adiye, vesi. Karuppi. Naaye. *Chi!* I'm calling you. Inje vaa-di!" I threw a tea towel at her.

"I don't know!" she shouted.

She stood from the floor and went to her room. Her slouching saddened me.

"Did Mark come early this morning? This must be from him, no?"

Anji lit another one of her tobacco sticks, indoors this time. I didn't realize how in love with Mark she must've been. Blinded by her heartbreak. Not seeing the blessing that lay in front of her. I didn't realize how worried my poor child was we wouldn't have the money for rent.

Faith would have saved her from her torment. There was money, thousands and thousands of dollars on our table, and my girls couldn't see that this was God's doing. This was a miracle.

"Mommy, Mommy. Mark on the TV, Mommy. Look at the fire, Mommy. Mommy. Look."

We ran to the living room, where Maysha pointed at the screen.

Witnesses were startled to see the house ablaze earlier this morning on Cherry Wood Lane in the East End of the city. An eyewitness was quick to call emergency services.

"It was almost a premonition, seeing the flames. I couldn't believe this was happening right in front of me. I heard about the wildfires and what to expect with the ozone layer and all of that, but I didn't expect it to happen so soon . . ."

Firefighters arrived too late at the scene and the remains of twenty-nine-year-old Jonathan Barnes have been identified. Neighbors are holding a vigil—

My heart shattered for that boy. Quickly, I found a seat on the couch.

"Mark wasn't even his real name?"

"Jesus Christ," mumbled Anji, walking off into the kitchen. *Walking off.*

"Anji! He's dead! He's dead! That's Mark's photo at the corner of the screen!"

Anji stopped in her tracks. She marched back to my side, pointing her skinny finger in my face.

"And what do you want me to do about it?"

"It was you. Was it you?"

"We rode home together, Mary. Don't ask me foolish questions."

"I heard a rustling, but I didn't think it was anything too suspicious. Just some racoons copulating, knocking over trash, or something. Some people are calling it a wildfire, some people think maybe that guy had it coming. He smoked a lot. Real strange guy. Almost set his garage on fire once. I never talked to the guy, but a guy's dead, and you could feel it."

I prayed. Right there on the couch. Crying in my hands. I prayed.

Anji made us tea and handed me one of her cigarettes.

DILO

We paid our landlord on the fifteenth of December. He would have come for his money at midnight if it didn't specifically state 9 a.m. pickup in our lease. He was a punctual man. I stood waiting in the front yard, bundled up tight, holding my machete. Secretly, I think he was unhappy to see we had the money. I waved at that cocksucker anyway.

On the seventeenth, we went to the Way of Truth Evangelical Church. Looking a lot more modest, I'd say. Looking more like ourselves. Anji wore one of my hoodies. Mary wore her yellow house robe. I wore a *South Park* sweater I'd found at the YMCA. Satan kissing Saddam Hussein.

The pastor said a few words for "our brother in the Lord's care, Jonathan 'Mark' Barnes." We sat in a full pew with the Original Batch. Most of them crying. The Five sat up closer to the front, as they normally did. The camera was all up in Sheila's face. She wore shades and a wide black-brimmed hat with a lace veil that covered her face. Sheila organized a fundraiser for SickKids in honor of Mark. Something about how Mark told her he volunteered there on Wednesdays. Teaching blind children to crochet. Sheila told people that Mark was a Good Samaritan.

"Church," the pastor started, wiping his mouth, "the Holy Spirit is speaking to me . . . Some of you have lost your faith in the Lord. Some of you have misplaced your faith in man. The Holy Spirit is angry, church! *Oh, shaba kee so fa!* The Lord God says! For man will always disappoint. For man is nothing without his master. And the Lord says, repent and find your way. Give to the Lord what He is due. Humble yourself onto your God, or He will have you cleaning a donkey's ass in the New Jerusalem. In Jesus's mighty name—glory hallelujah! Amen and amen."

The Original Batch, the Five, Mary, they were all devastated. Ruined. Dried prunes on a driveway. With Mark gone they lost their hopes and dreams. They also lost a whole load of cash, relatively speaking. I'm sure they loved the guy, but who wasn't excited about the next return?

By the nineteenth of December, the case on Cherry Wood Lane had been closed. Firefighters found the cigarette that had sparked Mark's tragedy. He was known to smoke a pack a day. Our biggest remaining problem was figuring out what to do with almost eighty-three G's. There was no way we were going to keep that much cash in our home. Even if Mark had had everyone sign a waiver. Even if the police weren't aware of any money Mark was connected to. *At that time,* at least.

Anji and I were forced to put our heads together. Forced to interact. We hadn't spoken since the day she almost killed me. We went to Mona's. Just the two of us.

"I know you know how to start fires. You're not in trouble, Dilo," she whispered.

"I already told you. I don't even know where he lives."

"Why can't you look me in the eye when you say so? Your eyes are darting all over the diner."

"It's busy in here. I want to go home, Anji. It's getting too loud."

She brushed crumbs off the table. Mona had sent over two bowls of soup and fresh garlic bread. The diner was decorated with Christmas lights and boughs of holly. Large red and green ornamental balls hung from the ceiling.

Anji picked at some bread.

"Well, I was thinking," she started. "We split the money. Without question. But not with the Five. That money is peanuts to them," she whispered.

"Sure. Whatever. But tell everyone Mark left a note. Or a will. Detailed instructions."

"Mark couldn't write a detailed note, let alone a bloody sentence." She laughed.

"Don't be a bitch, Anji. He's dead."

I looked in her eyes when I said it.

"Can we go now?" I asked.

Anji concocted a story that she shared with Mary and the members of the Original Batch. She called up each one of them on the phone in the kitchen. It took her the whole day.

And, well, that was it, really.

Where we came from, if someone shows up and offers you ten grand, you don't ask a bunch of questions.

The crucial part, what Anji had said Mark even underlined, in this *imaginary* will of his, was that the Original Batch were to never mention the money they received to anyone. Ever. Not even their families. The final stipulation was that not a dime of the ten grand should be given to God, either. The money was their blessing alone. In Jesus's name. Amen.

Like I've said from the start, people need something to believe in. Something to hang on to. Something they can call their own. The Original Batch were ecstatic Mark had cared so much about them. That he had protected them. Even in death. Mark died a hero. Mark died a man of God.

ANJI

I'd never know just how much money Mark had in circulation. I suspected that he'd had a group of investors before the Original Batch. But no one ever turned up looking for the money.

I can admit that I had made some mistakes. But I didn't intentionally plan to scam God's people. That wasn't my style. Mark ran a small scheme that I happened to get roped into, *which just so happened* to be at an Evangelical church.

I had contacts with connections to the PLO. I was a Tamil Tiger. A resistance fighter. If the state could kill their own people, deprive countless and many, there was no telling what more the state would do to us, at night, while we were sleeping. They may dream of annihilation. Obliterating our histories. Our people washed away from the sand to the seas, and—what will be done about it?

I fought for the liberation of my people, then I was forced to grapple with the concept of liberating the mind.

You see some good, and you come to know evil. "Terrorized" could never describe an ineffable experience. You see the world with a new pair of eyes, after you've fought on the front line with your gun, and then, as an act of resistance. There is a quote I can't quite recall, about thinkers as cowards, and fighters as fools. Anyway.

It could be I had a different view of the world. If *I* had planned a scam involving an Evangelical church, comrade, I'd have had a much bigger target. They are tax-exempt entities, after all. How many millions were fooled by the "gospel" of John Nelson Darby?

I knew absolutely nothing about the fire. About what had happened to Mark, I could only speculate, but I'd never know for certain. I worried about the possibility of the authorities watching us from unmarked cars parked on the roadside. But that wasn't a new fear of mine, and I had never let it stop me. I was learning how to live again. Learning how to live. I'll one day have answers, I'll one day have time. The time. I will one day have the time to breathe in a stillness I've never had before. That, I believed.

MARY

Recalling this time, my hands begin to tremble. The Way of Truth Evangelical Church built a new church. Cancún Dreams Worship Centre. The Five donated enough money for Pastor Todd to build not only his tabernacle but also all-inclusive cabins for members of the congregation and their guests.

I stopped attending, not long after Mark left us to be with our Lord. I was no longer a member. Those people didn't know the God I served. My God gave the ultimate sacrifice so we could live and care for each other. Preparing our hearts for His second coming. I didn't care about Louis Vuitton and Calvin Klein. Talking about Mercedeses and fancy dresses. I enjoyed simple things, no? Simple things and friendship. We had the love of the Original Batch. We had each other. Imagine the heartache if we were all left with nothing. If Mark truly left us all without a cent. *Chi!* If I lost my friends because of money, what another tragedy that would be. Ha! My hands aren't shaking as much now. Praise the Lord.

DILO

What if our use of the internet becomes the death of all that is meaningful? If all of earth's history were replayed, would it ever play out completely the same? In how many versions would we have Sudbury's crater? These were just a few of the questions I asked myself while I strolled the aisles at Z-Mart 416, as the newly hired loss prevention inspector. When you think no one's watching, somebody usually is.

My supervisor was an officer I'd never noticed before. A small Korean girl named Tammy. She was more discreet than a pregnant teenager hiding those first few weeks. Tammy was top tier and saw that I had some talent.

Who could resist the offer? Most people looked at me and thought I was trouble, a thief. A degenerate. A ghetto kid. Those were the cards I was dealt. Always having to look over my shoulder. Routinely harassed by adults. But now I was an upstanding member of society. I was not just legit but behind enemy lines.

I thought it would take some time getting comfortable before I found my footing. Thought I'd be working solo, actually. That first day, Tammy sat me down in our office; Loss Prevention had their own tiny room with a Chuck Norris poster taking up most of the wall space. Denim on denim. CAN'T BE BEATEN in bold yellow.

Tammy stooped in her chair, legs parted, hands together.

"Z-Mart is going bankrupt and will probably shut down in the next five years. Too many Wal-Sharts popping up. A few of us have a thing going. Just keep it clean if you want in. Can you manage that?"

I was living the dream.

We had guys moving contraband Krafty Kon product out of the store for their friends and family. We packed the goods in backpacks or boxes, depending on who was managing that night. Terrance was in on the deal, too. We'd fill up a guy's car at the loading dock, in the one area with a dead security camera. Tammy made sure most of the workers were taken care of. None of us were ever gonna be given a raise. The whole Z-Mart ship was tanking, but there was still money coming in, even if the board of directors thought otherwise. I saw tons of cash up there. You could build a school with the stacks I saw. We skimmed what we could. You start caring less when management's not working for your best interest. I even heard rumors that management received a bonus if they kept promotions down. The board of directors, the CEO, the founding father of this Z-Mart, they were all living bougie pimped-out lives. So, why shouldn't we live a little? No need to really give a damn. We were out there just trying to survive, maybe save up enough to splurge every now and then without having to feel the blow of missing money.

Did I have time to reflect on what happened? Give myself the time to think about that brief period of my life? That tiny little sliver? A month and a half, that was. Maybe three. No, not really. I had money to make. Straight A's to keep for my mother, Mary. Money on my mind. Family's gotta eat. I was doing just fine. I had big plans for myself. I still had my own dreams.

EPILOGUE

MAY 2004

Mary pulled off her hairnet in the women's locker area, catching a glimpse of herself in the mirror. Her hair was sweaty. Her curls defined. She emptied the contents of her lunch box in the garbage, realizing the few grapes she hadn't eaten were squished in the plastic sandwich bag. Her spoon and fork were sticky. She glanced at her watch and saw she had five minutes or so to leave and be on time. She moistened a few paper towels at the sink and wiped down the inside of her Tupperware before gathering up all her belongings. Her coat. Her backpack. She placed her steel-toe boots in her locker with her uniform and jacket. That afternoon she packed a box of broken chocolate chip cookies and deformed animal crackers to take home.

"See you tomorrow, A.J. Have a good night, crew."

Mary waved to her colleagues and signed out from her shift, flashing her Dino's Biscuit Factory ID on the scanner. Mary Naagadevi—floor supervisor in training.

Anji held a pair of tongs, picking out chocolate-glazed donuts and neatly lining them up on display. The plastic on the inside of her Tim Hortons visor scratched her skin annoyingly. Her colleague, a young woman in her late teens, held the tray still and steady. A new hire. She chomped a gob of gum on one side. Astutely watching Anji, who was crouched down beside the glass display.

"Is it true what people are saying about you?" she asked, looking out to see if there were any customers.

"What are people saying now?" asked Anji.

"Just that you dated the guy who invented the Iced Capp or something."

"Oh yeah. I gave him the damn idea too."

Anji glanced at the clock. A quarter of an hour to go before she'd meet Mary in the parking lot.

A man walked straight up to Anji's counter. She'd seen him every so often but was usually able to avoid his gaze.

"A double-double. Just one. Large."

Anji keyed in his selection.

"You're one of those that speaks English good. You lookin' like a tight tart today," he slurred, specks of spit flying from his mouth, landing on Anji's register, a drop on her arm.

Anji worked six days a week. Four of those days were spent as a support worker at Christy's House Women's Shelter, and two of those days were behind the counter at Tim Hortons. She loved the smell of coffee and chocolate in the morning and was hired because she emphasized how much she enjoyed meeting new people. In three weeks, she'd complete her part-time yoga training. She hoped to start her own class in another part of the city, where no one had ever seen her before. Guru Ji would be her name, and she was the daughter of a famous guru from Southern India, where she was born in the Kodayar forests. Guru Ji had the gift of spiritual wisdom that had been passed through her family for centuries. For fifty dollars an hour, she'd serve as a conduit for the forest gods, and the spirits were willing to whisper fortunes to yogis in pricey polyester gear. Anji was looking forward to those weeks ahead.

She walked over to her manager at the order station, leaving her customer unattended.

"I want to slap the man at my counter even after I counted down from five. Will you be a doll and take care of his order for me?"

Her purse over her shoulder, a box of Timbits in one hand and two Iced Capps on a carrying tray she held in the other, Anji pushed open the back door with her foot.

Mary grabbed the drinks from Anji as she settled in the passenger side. Anji yanked a denim shirt from her gym bag behind Mary's seat. Mary offered Anji a chunk of chocolate chip cookie, which Anji declined. She unbuttoned her Tim Hortons uniform and threw it in the back of the car, before buttoning up the denim long-sleeve, finally comfortable enough to have her drink.

"What took so long?" asked Mary.

"It's been two minutes since I clocked out."

Mary made a face and took a long sip of her drink, holding her head from the rush of ice. Her back hurt but she was looking forward to swimming in the late evening with her friends Tracey and Lina at the rec center. She fiddled with the radio, turning the volume down. She started the car.

From the elevator, Mary and Anji both knew to turn left. Mary had gone straight from work to the production studio, but she had begged to leave her post as guardian for a brief ten minutes, so she could give Anji a ride. The shoot had a hard stop at five. Waiting for Mary's return was a woman from the production team, holding a clipboard. She took Mary back on set, while Anji stayed by reception. A young woman with heavy eye makeup and glossy lips looked up from her desk.

"Lisa said I could double-check rates here. It's for Maysha Anjali, please."

"Absolutely! That's a thousand dollars for the day shoot, and let's see, that's an eight-thousand-dollar buyout with an option to renew for two years at a hundred and ten percent. We, like, really aim to keep our talent satisfied. That's totally our vision," the woman said with a strong vocal fry.

After settling up, Anji made her way to the well-lit set.

In front of a green screen, seated on a bar stool, with a box of Krafty Kon Kups—a new chocolate crunch breakfast cereal—on her lap, was Maysha. She smiled from ear to ear. Showing off her dimples. She was a natural and, most important, a true Krafty Kon evangelist. A woman finished powdering Maysha's nose. She waved seeing her mother and periyamma.

Anji and Mary watched from a couch in the back. Maysha insisted this was her dream. She adored being in front of the camera and had been working the lens for three years. The women waited patiently for the final take. For the director to call cut, so they could leave and settle into the end of the day.

It was nearly time to rest.

Dilo stood tall in short heels, scanning the beach hats on display. She had on red straight-leg trousers, ironed well at the seams, with a matching blazer. She wore small circular-framed shades, her hair in a sleek ponytail.

Z-Mart that early afternoon was calm, closing time only thirty agonizing minutes away. Dilo's eyes were on a woman in her late thirties. Nicely dressed. Mustard blouse. Tweed trousers and comfortable heels. She slipped a pack of highlighters into her purse. A couple packs of notepads. Washable markers, too. The woman took small steps. Looking over her shoulder every so often, glancing up at the ceiling. Scanning for cameras. As the woman drew nearer, Dilo realized she recognized her. Ms. Emma Lieberman, her former English teacher.

Emma perused aisles in the pricier pharmaceutical section.

Usually, Dilo would look the other way. Move on to another aisle in another section. Loss Prevention had its own jurisdictions, its own code of ethics. But Dilo found herself hot on Emma's heels out of curiosity. Careful to maintain a reasonable trailing distance so as to not raise suspicion. From Travel and Accessories, through Books, and by Boys' on the opposite side.

Emma scanned her blind spots. She quickly glanced over her shoulder and, seeing no one near, slid a bottle of B12 into her jacket. In Health and Beauty, Emma eyed the face serums enclosed in the locked display. She strolled as if interested in buying a bottle of lotion, but Dilo knew all the tricks. Emma's hands were dry, and perhaps she'd left her usual Lancôme lotion in her car. Scanning her peripheral vision, she twisted the cap off a tube of cucumber and melon hand cream, squirting a quarter-sized amount on her palms. Dilo tapped her shoulder from behind.

"Hi, miss."

"Oh my God! You scared me. Dilo? You look fantastic. Are you working now or are you still in school?"

"Second year of uni, miss. Criminology and international law is what I'm thinking. Not sure yet."

"Wow. Okay. I can see that. Amazing."

"Thanks. That cream smells good."

"This? Oh, yes, it smells lovely. Was just picking it up. Shame Z-Mart is closing down in a week. Our students are devastated."

"For sure. Our Z-Mart in Malvern Mall? It's iconic. Everyone in Scarborough knows that. But hey! Congrats on your romance trilogy, miss, I heard it's doing pretty well."

Dilo revealed a copy she had hidden behind her back. Marked with several stickers. A yellow "Buy One Get One Half Off" under a red "50% off" clearance sticker.

"Oh my, thank you, Dilo. That is so sweet of you to say. Did you find this here?"

"In the local authors section, yeah. I heard one of the sales managers was an old student of yours. Made management grab copies."

"That's so nice to know, actually. Authors don't make much at all for all the work they do, but I'm best teaching literature, anyway," she laughed, her cheeks flushed, her nose red.

"What was your elevator pitch again? Danielle Steel meets Jane Austen?"

"You remember?"

"You spoke about your novel practically every day."

"That's why it's great to have a passion."

"And you achieved a dream."

"When you put in the time and hard work . . ."

"You self-published, right?"

"Yeah, it was challenging querying for agents. Publishers don't want to take risks these days. But I made this happen for myself, and, you know what? It feels great."

"That's pretty awesome, miss. Any crazy book tours?"

"The school organized a nice gathering at Mona's just down the road."

"So well deserved. Probably going to see your name in big flashing lights soon. Maybe a movie deal?"

"Ha. Maybe. So, are you still writing?"

"No. Oh no. Better off keeping my opinions to myself."

Dilo laughed. Emma brushed a strand of hair from her face. Unsure, she feigned a smile.

"I started journaling, though. For when things pop into my head."

"That's excellent, dear. I know you were part of the group that used to freestyle in the stairwell. Not a safe place to do so, but I was proud we had that kind of talent at our school."

"Our open mic. Yeah, I did some spoken word. Just once, though. Got suspended for three days because of a poem—"

"Were you? Oh dear. Explicit content, perhaps? I don't know. But you're in university now! And looking great, Dilo. A real woman, so grown and polished. I'm proud of you." Emma smiled with tight lips, her eyes squished into slits. "I wish you the very best, dear."

She touched Dilo's arm and waved goodbye, carrying on with her shopping.

Dilo made her rounds, saddened it was one of her last few shifts. Though she still gave her job her all. She eyed Terrance at his post. He nodded, acknowledging her gesture.

Ms. Lieberman walked casually toward the exit, smiling at the people passing by in Z-Mart store 416. She looked forward to the coming end of the school year. Soon she'd be enjoying a mug of tea with her cat, Chloe, on her chaise. Step after step, nearing the exit, she smiled at Terrance and made it past the sensors without the alarm sounding. But Terrance waddled over from his post with his hand held out in front of him.

"Excuse me, ma'am. Would you mind coming with me?"

Dilo watched from Books, standing by the novel section, with a smile on her face.

ACKNOWLEDGMENTS

This novel drove me through forms of madness, but not suicide or murder. For all that I experienced while writing, for all that I drew upon. For all that I contemplated about our humanity, our species and our times, for all we were witness to—writing from September 2023 to the end of 2025. I worried about my depleting funds and my mental health, having been in an isolation I've never experienced, even as the loner I am.

2 Timothy 3:1-5

I am grateful to myself for pushing through and finishing. To all the small things that kept me going. Psychedelics and lisdexamfetamine. To creatine and veggie hot dogs. To Greek yogurt with no added sugar and cans of black beans. To protein powder, blueberries, and taco stands around Manzanillo. To long walks and my legs. To sunrises in Basingstoke and sunsets in Texas. To all the love I have in Toronto. To Scarborough. To the places and species I've had the honor of experiencing, especially while writing this novel.

Hebrews 13:5

To Khari Dawkins, Rachel Imrie, and Deborah Sun de le Cruz. To Rita Madrigal. To Cara Riley and Joanna Lee. Thank you all for your hand, mind, and time. Thank you Khari for your patience and insight. Thank you for asking the right questions.

James Roxburgh, Alice Latham, David Forrer, and the entire team at Atlantic Books.

Michael Goldberg, Anne Jaconette, Laura Gonzalez, and the entire team at Doubleday and Penguin Random House. To Aruna Dahanayake. To Sebastian Godwin.

Emily Mahon and Nada Hayek for my cover design, another work of art.

To Nedra Rodrigo for the Tamil transliteration—for your care and time.

To friends in Sri Lanka, and all I've learned about a place called Back Home. To my chiththa and aunty. Maamas and maamis, chiththis and chiththas, uncles and aunties—to my elders. To the land where I was born and the places I've lived. To the palmyra (*borassus flabellifer*) and flying foxes. To the singing fish too.

To friends who checked in, loved, and fed me. For being there. Alyia Ibrahim, Khadija, Katie, Golshan Abdmoulaie, Ramiya Pushparajah, Zo, Ehab, and N.W. To my neighbors Priya and Danielle. To G.K. To Daniel Renwick. To Joey Santore. To the good, bad, and ugly. To Juan.

To my loves Zaha and Salah, always. To the vets who saved Z's life during the week when my final draft was due.

To the baristas who made me cups of coffee.

To the book world, and all the hands that have helped produce physical copies, and then the hands that ship and send those copies out. I wish you all the very best.

To past readers, and those who've sent messages. To you, dear reader, whether I've kept your attention or not.

To anyone who's been scammed, conned, or slighted. May your heart, health, and/or bank balances heal tenfold, in Jesus's name.

To survivors of terror, abuse, and tragedy.

Isaiah 5:20

And finally, to my family. For your trust and love. For everything. I love you.

Acts 2:44–45

ABOUT THE AUTHOR

Priya Guns is the author of the critically acclaimed novel *Your Driver Is Waiting*. A former teacher, she is an actor and an arborist in training whose previous work has been published in short story anthologies, *gal-dem, Spring* magazine, and anonymously in *The Guardian*.